"You stood me up."

"I never agreed to a date. You shouldn't make assumptions," Harper said.

Teagan chuckled, taking careful note of how a subtle shiver rocked her body. "Caught a chill?" he teased, knowing full well it wasn't a chill that caused her to shake. "Lucky for you, all's well that ends well. I have an open spot at my table for you."

Teagan released her and moved in front, daring her to turn him down.

She met his gaze with a subtle smile playing on her lips. "Maybe I'm already meeting someone."

"You are. Me."

"Not you," she said with a small laugh. "Someone else."

"Impossible."

"Your ego is quite healthy, isn't it?"

"So is my libido."

Color flushed her cheeks a pretty pink. "What makes you think I'm interested in you like that?"

Teagan reached over to lightly caress the goose bumps still rioting on her arm. "Because your body tells m

Dear Reader,

I love witty banter. If a scene between characters can make me laugh, I know it's a keeper. But even better than creating winning banter is a story that can make me laugh *and* cry—now, that's a real success.

I confess, I did cry at the end of this story. Hot, sexy, emotional, funny...*Tempted* is the entire package and I hope you agree.

I won't lie—I struggled with this book. Not because I didn't love the story or the characters but because I wanted to do them justice. I wanted to ensure that my readers experienced the full gamut of emotion that happens between two stubborn people who are determined to have their own way but ultimately realize that sometimes when you win, you lose.

Anyway, please enjoy and if you did, tell a friend! Or drop me a line and tell me what you thought.

I love hearing from readers. Connect with me on Facebook, Twitter or drop me an email. Or you can also write me a letter at PO BOX 2210, Oakdale, CA 95361.

Kimberly

Kimberly Van Meter

—

Tempted

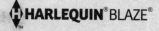

HARLEQUIN® BLAZE®

Recycling programs
for this product may
not exist in your area.

ISBN-13: 978-0-373-79958-9

Tempted

Copyright © 2017 by Kimberly Sheetz

Printed in U.S.A.

www.Harlequin.com

Kimberly Van Meter wrote her first book at sixteen and finally achieved publication in December 2006. She writes for the Harlequin Superromance, Blaze and Romantic Suspense lines. She and her husband of seventeen years have three children, three cats, and always a houseful of friends, family and fun.

Books by Kimberly Van Meter

Harlequin Blaze

The Hottest Ticket in Town
Sex, Lies and Designer Shoes
A Wrong Bed Christmas
"Ignited"
The Flyboy's Temptation

Harlequin Romantic Suspense

The Sniper
The Agent's Surrender
Moving Target
Deep Cover
The Killer You Know

Harlequin Superromance

Family in Paradise

Like One of the Family
Playing the Part
Something to Believe In

The Sinclairs of Alaska

That Reckless Night
A Real Live Hero
A Sinclair Homecoming

To get the inside scoop on Harlequin Blaze and its talented writers, visit Facebook.com/BlazeAuthors.

All backlist available in ebook format.

Visit the Author Profile page at Harlequin.com for more titles.

To all those brave souls who open their hearts to the most wonderful and terrifying adventures one can have in life...I wish you the courage to try and the strength to hold on.

"Love is the voice under all silences, the hope which has no opposite in fear; the strength so strong mere force is feebleness: the truth more first than sun, more last than star."

— E. E. Cummings

1

Former air force pilot Teagan Carmichael didn't do cruises.

And yet, here he was, handing his boarding pass to the attendant, about to board the *Nautica* cruise liner, still a little unsure as to how his brother, J.T., had convinced him this was a good idea.

Mexico of all places. Two months ago, he and his buddies were flying into South America to rescue his brother J.T. after he'd accepted a charter flight gig to Mexico that had started out simple enough, but had ended up with J.T. and his female passenger crash-landing near the Guatemalan border.

They'd ended up in Sao Paulo, and somehow, by the grace of God, they'd made it out alive with all fingers and toes still intact, but Teagan was fairly certain luck had been a factor.

Maybe their guardian angels had cashed in some chips, because there were times Teagan had been fairly certain their goose was cooked.

Against all odds, they'd managed to not only escape, but to come out on top, which was the biggest surprise of all.

J.T. had made a lot of boneheaded decisions, but hiring on with Dr. Hope Larsen had been an unexpected blessing in several different ways.

"Welcome aboard, Mr. Carmichael," the sharply dressed

male attendant said as he scanned the ticket electronically. "Enjoy your stay aboard the *Nautica*."

Gulls squawked a racket, screeching at one another as dirty waves lapped at the dock, the smell of brine salting the air. Los Angeles harbors weren't known for their beauty, but then no one was flocking to LA for the beaches, either.

Teagan nodded and walked up the gangplank to board the massive liner. Like most cruise ships, it was a city on water with every amenity, every luxury.

Bright pennant flags flapped in the wind, snapping like colorful towels, signaling something festive was about to happen on this boat, but Teagan was still questioning his decision to go through with the cruise.

He probably could've talked his buddies Kirk Addler or Harris McGoy into taking the cruise instead, but J.T. had felt strongly about Teagan going, so he'd caved.

And thanks to the fat payment from Tessara Pharmaceuticals from J.T.'s last charter—the one that'd subsequently trashed their only plane and nearly gotten them all killed—Teagan was staying in an upgraded stateroom.

"Well, aren't you a tall drink of water." An older, curvy, auburn-haired goddess wearing a fancy outfit and dripping with rings, was eyeing him with open appreciation. "If you're representing what we have to look forward to on this singles cruise, then I'm all in, sugar."

Oh, that's another thing. J.T. had booked him on a cruise meant for hooking up.

Like Teagan needed a relationship right now. With rebuilding Blue Yonder Charter, revamping their business plan and generally trying to start over, he didn't have time for slap and tickle on a regular basis.

Teagan chuckled, blushing only slightly because attention from a beautiful woman, even one considered a cougar, was still flattering as hell. But he wasn't looking for a hook-up. No matter what J.T.'s advice had been before dropping him off at the dock.

"You need to loosen up, big brother," J.T. had said, admonishingly. "You're wound tighter than a drum. You'd think that almost dying would've reminded you that life is for the living."

"You're giving me advice?" Teagan had joked. "Is this a sign of the coming apocalypse?"

Because, yeah, Teagan was the cool head and J.T. was the screwup.

At least, J.T. was until he'd met that saucy redhead scientist, Hope. Now his little brother was becoming responsible and thinking with his head and not his…well, you know.

And maybe Teagan had been a little bit envious of how happy J.T. was with Hope, but seeing as he wasn't about to do anything to change his relationship status, there wasn't much he could do about that.

The woman gave Teagan a final, bold up-down appraisal and then clucked her tongue with approval as she sashayed down the hallway to find her own room.

That was definitely a cougar sighting.

And a pretty fine one at that.

But as he found his room, his neighbor found hers and he forgot all about the cougar.

Teagan wasn't much of a believer of insta-love but he was a big fan of insta-lust, and he'd just been hit square between the eyes with a double dose.

Long dark hair curled in lazy loops and waves to the small of her back, shapely, tan legs that went on for days and the most pert, rounded breasts that he craved to touch—all he could do was stare like an idiot.

Deep blue eyes framed by incredibly lush black lashes met his stunned gaze and she graced him with a sly smile, as if she knew good and well just how primal her effect was on men.

This was a level ten hottie and she knew it.

A tremor of excitement rocked his spine as his insides

did a weird tumble and roll. To be truthful, he'd never been so knocked on his ass by a single look.

He'd been around the world and seen plenty of gorgeous, exotic women but every single one of them paled in his memory the minute he saw her.

And then she was gone.

One coy look and she disappeared behind her door.

He didn't know her name.

Didn't know anything about her.

But he would.

Suddenly, this cruise was the best idea ever.

He'd have to thank J.T. for forcing him to take the trip, because he'd just stared into the eyes of his destiny.

Or at the very least, his next adventure.

He was down for either.

HARPER RILEY CLOSED the door behind her, her heart dancing a flurried tippety-tap at the enigmatic stranger with the arresting eyes and magnificent build.

With all that solid muscle and those rugged good looks, he probably knew how to make a woman forget her own name.

Probably a player.

Most beautiful people were.

Not that she held that against him.

Hell, Harper played with the best of them.

But, whoa, she'd have to steer clear of that man for the duration of her trip.

This wasn't a pleasure cruise for her.

It was work.

Her target was Stuart Buck, recently widowed, incredibly wealthy.

And very vulnerable.

Harper had plans to become the next Mrs. Stuart Buck. She'd been tracking the older man's activities for months. Harper knew everything that needed to be known about him.

A self-starter, Stuart was responsible for the rubber flush valve inside toilets. Not very glamorous, but mega lucrative, because everyone used toilets, right?

And while Harper didn't love the idea of becoming Mrs. Toilet Queen, she'd probably just have to console herself by spending all that lovely toilet money.

So why was a multimillionaire hitching a ride on a commercial liner when he probably had a handful of yachts at his disposal?

Well, Stuart liked to think of himself as an everyman's man. As in, he liked to surround himself with people who were still hungry, made him think he was still one of them.

Even though he wasn't.

But Harper didn't begrudge the old man his illusions. Everyone had something they liked to hold on to.

The plan was a relatively straightforward, if not classic, old-school seduction.

Stuart was still mourning his wife, but her death wasn't so fresh that Stuart would find Harper's interest offensive.

In Harper's experience, men were simple creatures. At their core, they needed to be wanted, they needed someone to coo and aww over their accomplishments and laugh at their jokes.

A man was putty in a woman's hands if she knew how to work those basic triggers.

And Harper had honed her skills to a knife point.

Tonight was the mixer dinner where she would set the plan in motion.

Everything was planned down to the smile. Seduction was about more than just dressing the part—it was making a calculated decision to steer conversations, reacting to body language and adjusting accordingly.

She mentally went over her game plan, ticking off items

on her to-do list as she usually did before going after her target.

But this time, her neighbor kept interrupting her thoughts.

Harper frowned when she couldn't quite stay on task.

The warning tingle in the pit of her belly should've been enough to shut down any meandering thoughts about the alluring stranger, but there was something about that man— jeez, she'd only caught a glimpse—that wouldn't let loose.

And it was seriously messing with her game day ritual.

He was obviously single and ready to mingle.

Even though he was hot as hell and probably a fun time in the sack, Harper wouldn't indulge.

A pretty face was a lie she couldn't afford.

Her mother might not have absorbed the lesson in time but Harper sure as hell had—pretty mouths spewed convenient lies.

And now her mother was in a care facility without a cent to her name, because someone had fleeced her out of her savings with promises he'd never intended to keep.

Harper shook off the distasteful memories and hardened herself to the budding attraction that'd had the gall to spring up uninvited within her.

In another life, Harper could definitely see herself pressed up against all that lovely man-meat, but not today.

One glance and she could already tell he wasn't worth her time.

He had that blue-collar ruggedness about him. Wind-chapped cheeks meant he worked outside in some capacity, or spent a lot of time skiing or sailing, but his hands were big and strong as if he was accustomed to hard work.

The man could probably bend her into a pretzel, but he couldn't keep her in riches.

So, sorry, Mr. Cutie-pie, not going to happen.

Harper sighed. *Oh, well.* Time to focus on Mr. Buck.

Thin, bearded and balding Mr. Buck.

Just think of all that wonderful money.

2

TEAGAN CLOSED THE door to his stateroom, still thinking about the hottie with the body next door.

A cursory glance around the room confirmed it was nice—luxurious even—but he was more interested in getting to know why a woman like her was on a singles cruise, much less *single*.

Yeah, because let's face it...you get a girl like that...you lock that shit down tight.

Not that he was a caveman or anything, but a woman with smoking curves like hers could turn any levelheaded man into a ground-pounding, chest-thumping gorilla.

Maybe J.T. had booked him on a...swingers cruise or something. Like that trip in Jamaica where all the people in a certain lifestyle flocked to get their groove on.

J.T. had mentioned he wanted Teagan to "whoop it up," whatever that meant. And knowing J.T., that could mean virtually anything.

Plus J.T. would laugh his balls off sending Teagan on a swingers cruise without his knowledge.

A laugh a minute, little brother.

God, he hoped not.

He wasn't the sharing type.

And J.T. knew that.

Okay, let's go out on a limb and assume that J.T. is not that big of an asshole—particularly to the brother who'd saved his ass in Mexico—*and safely assume that this cruise is exactly as it was booked.*

Singles looking to mingle.

Ugh. He cringed at the very idea of walking around, acting like a horny dog, sniffing after eligible ladies in the hopes of a hook-up.

"J.T., you're an ass," he muttered, glancing around the room, wondering what his next step was. Was he supposed to do something? Go somewhere?

Was there an itinerary?

Teagan checked the nightstand, the bathroom and the small coffee table but found nothing to tell him what was in store for the next week. He sure as hell didn't want to sit around twiddling his thumbs in his room.

It was bad enough he was going to be floating around without any work to keep him busy, but the threat of completely idle time gave him the willies.

His gaze traveled to the opposite wall, knowing Little Miss Hot Stuff was on the other side.

Either fate had one damn fine sense of humor or was a mean bitch, because that woman was going to be hard to put out of his mind.

Teagan didn't know anything about her aside from the fact that he wanted to know her better.

But there was something cheesy about knocking on his neighbor's door with such an obvious pickup line, right?

Well, she did board a singles cruise, so that implied she was interested in meeting up with people, he reasoned.

Or maybe she'd been roped into this gig, same as Teagan, and just wanted to get through it.

Guess there was only one way to find out.

Hell, there was no harm in being friendly.

Teagan smoothed his hair and then exited his room to knock on his neighbor's door.

She opened it with a subtle frown until she saw him. "Yes?" A slow quizzical smile followed, and he started stuttering like a jackass who'd never been around a female in his life.

"Uh, so here's the thing… I have no idea what I'm supposed to be doing. And…forgive me if I sound like a perv, but…is this by any chance a swingers cruise?"

Way to lead with something nonthreatening, dude.

Her smile faltered but she didn't slam the door in his face—good sign—then answered, "No, it's for singles. Why? Were you looking for a swingers cruise?"

"No, not all!" Teagan smiled with relief. "Thank God. I'm not into that swapping business. I mean, no judgment for those who are, but I'm not the type who enjoys sharing."

"Good to know," she said, mildly amused. "Was there anything else…?"

Well, he was batting a thousand. Had he completely forgotten how to flirt?

Apparently.

The rust was practically grinding his gears. At one time, he'd been damn near the cat's meow. Now he couldn't even make simple conversation. Oh, how the mighty had fallen.

Time for some damage control.

"My brother booked this cruise for me and I'm…sort of flying blind," he said by way of apology.

A spark of reluctant interest lit up her blue eyes. "Does your brother always book your vacations?"

"Hell no. I don't usually have time to vacation, but even if I did, I wouldn't let J.T. take on that job. He and I have different ideas of what constitutes fun."

She crossed her arms lightly as if amused. "So why did your brother book you on a singles cruise?"

"It's not a story you want to hear standing in a hallway. It's more of an over-dinner conversation," he said with a grin. "Maybe with some wine, good food, excellent company."

"Oh, is that so?" she said, one eyebrow lifting. "And what makes it worth all that?"

Teagan held up three fingers then said, "Three words— *plane crash*, *corporate intrigue* and *danger*."

"I see math is not your strong suit."

"I don't know… I can count quite clearly how you plus me equals a cozy dinner for two. How about it? I know you want to hear this story."

She laughed. "No doubt you're the hero in this tale."

"I don't mean to brag, but I did my part."

"Let me guess, you're a covert operative in the CIA and you were on a super secret international mission," she teased, clearly not buying an ounce of his story. The irony was that his story was absolutely true. Although, he wasn't supposed to talk about it. Confidentiality and all that.

"Sorry to disappoint, but not the CIA," Teagan said with a half grin. "Just a private pilot with a charter who got lucky. Or unlucky, depending on how you look at it."

"Where'd you learn to fly?"

"The US Air Force."

"Hmm."

Usually that sentence prompted more interest. He wasn't one to use his service to open doors or drop panties, but he was a bit surprised by her lack of reaction. "Got bad history with a flyboy?" Teagan asked.

"No. Not at all. I just don't like people lying about time in the service. Some things should be sacred."

Teagan lost his smile. She thought he was lying? That was a new one. He straightened, quick to set her mind at ease, because it didn't sit right to be accused of doing something he abhorred. "You're right," he agreed, seeming to surprise her with his firm tone. "People who lie about serving their country are the lowest scum and I can assure you, there is no stolen valor here. I served my country willingly, as did my brother. Now we own a private charter plane business here in Los Angeles."

"What is your name?"

"Teagan Carmichael. And yours?"

Again that enigmatic smile but no reciprocal answer.

"Not gonna share?" he asked, drinking in every bit of her. She was so pretty, looking at her nearly hurt his eyes. There was something so untouchable about her, like a queen gracing her people with a glance and a subtle wave. "Seems kinda the point of this trip, right? Getting to know people?"

At that, she answered, "Harper Riley," and he nearly crowed with happiness. He had a name!

"Nice to meet you, Harper."

"Likewise, Teagan."

They were off to a decent start.

"So…about that dinner…"

But Harper wasn't as charmed as Teagan had thought because she flat out turned him down.

And then she closed the door firmly in his face.

Well, hell, that was not a good sign at all.

HARPER CLOSED THE door with a frown.

Why were the charming ones always broke as hell?

His idea of a good time probably included a monster truck rally and convenience store hot dogs.

Definitely not to her standard.

But, he was certainly nice to look at.

Damn, when was the last time she got to choose based on chemistry?

Boohoo, life's rough. Stop crying and start focusing.

Stuart Buck was the real prize.

Vulnerable, looking for someone to share his life with and hopefully old-fashioned when it came to prenups—as in he didn't believe in them.

Harper pulled her phone from her purse to refresh her mind with all the research she had archived on the old billionaire.

His wife, Rachel, had been the quintessential silent partner, standing behind her man as he'd built his empire, smiling with adoration at the man who'd revolutionized the toilet industry.

Props to you, Rachel, Harper thought with derision. *I could never do that.*

Harper was more about the end game than the building game.

And Stuart was nicely set up.

He owned property in the Hamptons, a Manhattan apartment, a log cabin in Vail and, of course, his palatial mansion on Nob Hill in San Francisco, as well as his well-appointed beach house in Santa Barbara.

An excited tingle tickled her stomach. She loved the thrill of the hunt, especially when the prize was fat and juicy like Stuart.

Harper would do her best to help Stuart move on from the death of Perfect Wifey Number 1.

Because life was for the living.

And it wasn't as if his wife was going to spend his millions.

A small smile found her, but, in spite of her plans to go over her research, Harper's thoughts drifted to her cute neighbor.

She certainly knew that type. Teagan Carmichael was the kind of man her mother would've tripped all over herself to land. But even if Anna Riley had never learned, Harper had gotten the message loud and clear.

Charming men were the first to bail when things got tough—or when they'd taken everything there was to take.

Poor Mom. In love with being in love. Eternally hopeful that the next guy was the one.

Harper would watch as men walked in and out of Anna's life, leaving her with less and less.

If a man had bad credit, was nearly homeless, with a string of abandoned baby mamas, but could charm her with a seemingly devoted smile, Anna was all in.

But if Anna was continually blinded by love, Harper had become jaded by it.

Especially after Rex Harrington. Or whatever his name truly was.

Just the thought of Rex and what he'd done to her mother—and by proxy, her—made Harper want to throw something.

So, it didn't matter that Teagan was the kind of man who took her breath away. His cute face and tight behind weren't going to pay her bills.

Tonight was the dinner and dance mixer. She'd already arranged to be seated at Stuart's table. No doubt she'd have to fend off her share of competition, but this wasn't her first rodeo.

She pulled up Stuart's picture. Not bad looking. Bald but not fat—that was a plus.

Her last target had been as jolly as Santa Claus in the waistband, but not quite as pleasant in his demeanor.

She tried not to remember the times when his slobbery kisses had nearly made her retch.

Ulysses Prawner had been the worst.

A millionaire, but barely so, he'd liked to spend his money on women and toys. Harper had helped him in his endeavors.

Only, Ulysses hadn't known when to stop. His investments couldn't keep up with his spending and before long he'd come to Harper with a sob story.

"Baby," he'd implored as she'd packed her bags. "I'm just in a slump. Things will get better. They always do. Don't go."

Harper had already been casing the next target and was eager to move on. Actually, she'd been relieved to find a reason to bail. "Ulysses, let's not make this uncomfortable. What we had has run its course."

"But I love you, baby," he'd cried, grasping for her hands.

She'd tried to find an ounce of compassion for the man, but the well had run dry.

Pulling her hands free, she'd cast him a look filled with pity and walked out the door.

Not empty-handed, of course.

Every gift, every bit of cash that flowed her way had gone into a secret account, as did all her investments.

Someday she'd have enough to be solvent on her own. No more chasing after wealthy old pricks, swallowing her dignity and pride to cater to their every whim.

Someday.

That's why Stuart Buck was so important.

That old man was going to put a ring on her finger— without the protection of a prenup.

Then, when he died, all of his assets would go to Harper.

No more scouring the society pages, frequenting country clubs and pretending to be someone she wasn't just to make a dollar.

No more stressing about how she was going to pay her mother's care bill.

The woman was as dependent on Harper as a child was on its parent.

Irony at its finest.

Even as much as Harper was focused on the big picture, there were times when a forlorn sadness intruded on her thoughts.

She'd stopped feeling guilty a long time ago, but now and then, she wished she had the luxury of enjoying a normal relationship.

Thankfully, that kind of wistful thinking didn't happen often, but seeing someone like Teagan was always good for a little melancholy.

The fact was, she didn't want to rely on anyone but herself for her well-being. In this world, either you were on the bottom or the top. And she made sure she was never on the bottom.

Harper jerked a short breath in and refocused. "Stuart, you sweet, old man. You are never going to know what hit you."

Harper slipped her phone back into her purse and disappeared into her bathroom to get ready.

The stage was set and the players ready.

Time for the performance.

3

Teagan surveyed the resplendent lounge, with burgundy walls and gold filigree ornamentation spilling out over every surface, and wondered if he'd somehow stepped into a time warp.

Lounge acts always reminded him of cheesy pickup lines and boozed-out singers looking for some last-ditch effort to rekindle their dying career.

In other words, Teagan had never really considered a lounge a great place to meet people he wanted to hang with.

But as his gaze perused the room, he locked on to the one person who'd made this trip remotely interesting.

Harper.

Long dark hair curled in lazy waves down her open-back black dress, the short hem teasing the toned length of her legs perched on sassy heels. Everything about her was elegant and refined, yet pulsed with a raw sensuality that spoke his language.

For him, everyone else faded away, even the flock of men surrounding her, all vying for a smile from the beauty.

Harper knew the power she held over men. Teagan could see it in the way she played the coy and delicate lady for the decidedly older men salivating around her.

He continued to watch with interest, finding the scene telling.

Teagan knew women of all kinds.

Being a former flyboy, his education on women had taught him that they could rule the world if they wanted.

They held the power in their nimble fingers to twist men in pretzels, but only a small percentage actually knew how to wield that power with any kind of efficiency.

But watching Harper, it was easy to see that the woman knew exactly what she was doing.

Good sense told him to walk away.

Find a different lady to spend his week with—someone less complicated.

Less dangerous.

But he knew that wasn't going to happen.

A slow burn of a smile spread on his lips. Harper was a challenge that fired him up in ways he hadn't allowed himself to feel in a long time.

But if he remembered the rules of this game correctly, a direct approach would end in failure.

Harper was all about strategy, cunning.

So he had to respond in kind.

Well, J.T. had wanted him to cut loose, have fun.

What better fun could there be than trying to catch a woman intent on running away?

Hell, it was a bad idea—practically reeking of disaster— but he was in.

All in.

Tonight's event was a standard meet and greet, with a single-and-ready-to-mingle vibe. Polite laughter and the buzz of conversation floated around the room. There were plenty of fish in this fishbowl, that was for certain.

Once his buddy Kirk Addler had joked that Teagan ought to put himself on Tinder. Teagan hadn't paid attention to the newest apps and whatnot that were out there, so he'd reluctantly checked it out, seeing as Kirk seemed keen on it.

After a few appalling swipes, Teagan was a definite *no*.

And Kirk deserved a kick in the ass.

And more than likely, an STD check.

Swipe right, swipe left…no thanks.

If that was the dating in the new age, he'd happily remain single.

Ignoring the urge to insert himself into her circle of admirers, Teagan made a deliberate detour to the bar but managed to make brief eye contact with the brunette hottie. However, he made sure he was the one to break contact first before continuing on, as if she were merely a blip on his ever-roving radar.

Chicks hated to be overlooked.

Especially ones who knew they were the hottest in the room.

A smartly dressed bartender politely attended to his needs and, after receiving his beer, he tipped the man well.

Teagan didn't have to wait long before his bait caught a nibble.

But not by the right fish.

Cougar Lady was hot on his trail, eyes flashing and tail twitching. "There you are again," she said, sliding into the seat beside him at the bar. This time she extended her hand in a seductive introduction. "Vanessa Vermuelen. And you are? Aside from tall, delicious and ready-to-eat?"

"Teagan Carmichael," he answered, appreciating the view of her bountiful cleavage practically inviting him to lay his head on it. He flagged the bartender, and because Teagan had tipped well, the bartender was eager to serve. "My lady friend here is in need of a drink."

"Whiskey sour," she said with a throaty laugh that was deep and sexy. Then she gently tugged at the bartender's sleeve and said with a wink, "And don't go light on the whiskey, sweet thing."

The bartender grinned and ducked his head in a nod. "You got it."

Vanessa turned to Teagan. "The drinks are included in your package but they tend to skimp on the good stuff. I always like to let the bartender know that I like a *stiff*...drink."

If Teagan hadn't been clued in already, he would've caught the message loud and clear this time—he was on her meal plan.

"So tell me, Teagan... What are you here for?" she asked, going for the direct approach. "A little fun, something deeper? Because I'm open to either. I'm footloose and fancy-free and I intend to live it up."

Teagan couldn't help but smile at the engaging woman, even if he didn't want to sleep with her. She had a way about her that was infectious, and he liked her company.

"I'm not sure what I'm looking for," he answered. "My brother booked this cruise and kinda forced me to go."

"Sounds like a fun brother," she said, sipping her drink. "So, not married? Divorced? Widowed? What's your story?"

"Absolutely single. Never been married. You?"

Vanessa released a breath in dramatic style and readjusted her ample cleavage. "Was married to a real son of a bitch but he did me a solid and died. His insurance payout was about the only decent thing he ever did in his life."

"That bad, huh?"

"He wasn't winning any humanitarian awards," Vanessa drawled with derision, then tacked on, "Well, I stayed with the bastard too long so that's my fault, but I was raised that you didn't quit. So I stayed. Wasted the best parts of my life, too. But that's over, honey. I'm here to tear things up, starting with you, sugar pot." She squeezed his thigh, and he jumped. Her eyes lit up as she grinned. "You are a jumpy thing. All that young energy, stamina...mmm...just what I am looking for."

Teagan didn't want to hurt the older lady's feelings, but he didn't want to lead her on, either. "Vanessa, you are a smoking-hot woman, no doubt. Some man is going to be counting his lucky stars with you on his arm but I'm not sure I'm ready to take things to that level."

Vanessa's smile was strained around the edges but she nodded. "Sure, no problem. You're old-fashioned. I like that. Most times men are just eager to drop their drawers if the invitation is bold enough."

"When did your husband die?" he asked.

She exhaled before taking another drink. "Two years ago. Heart attack. Dropped dead in the middle of a steak dinner. Ruined everyone's appetite, that's for sure. I haven't been back to that restaurant since."

Even though Vanessa implied she was glad to be widowed, Teagan sensed lingering grief. Some things were hard to quit, especially if it was something like a long-term relationship.

"So, I do these cruises for fun, to pass the time. Meet people."

"How many cruises have you done?" he asked.

"This is my fourth."

Four singles cruises? Basically, two a year for the past two years since her husband died. That admission told a story.

"What was your husband's name?"

She cast him an uncertain look as if surprised he was asking, then answered, "Dale. We were high school sweethearts."

Vanessa blinked rapidly and Teagan realized she was fighting tears. Fluttering her hands to wipe away any moisture before it left a track down her heavily made-up face, she rose and excused herself before Teagan could say anything.

Maybe Dale hadn't been as rotten as Vanessa liked to say.

Sometimes being angry was easier than accepting the pain of true grief.

So far this meet and greet was not going well.

Maybe he could find another woman and send her off in tears.

He motioned for the bartender. "Keep 'em coming."

HARPER KNEW THE minute Teagan entered the room. It was as if her eyes were set to track and her aim was unerring.

He looked good.

Damn good.

That self-assured swagger as he surveyed the room, the way a smile flirted with his mouth…he was a bad distraction.

She knew she ought to flirt with the cluster of men corralling her, but seeing as Stuart was a no-show, the idea of wasting time with those pitiful fools was more than she could stomach.

The smart thing would be to return to her room, rest up for tomorrow.

But she wasn't tired.

In fact, she was practically brimming with restless energy and if she went to her room right now, she'd end up pacing a hole in her tiny stateroom.

A drink would take the edge off.

Don't do it. Don't you dare walk over to him.

Ignoring the voice of reason, she politely extricated herself from the cluster and made her way toward Teagan.

She slid into the chair that'd been occupied by the older woman and smiled at the bartender. "Gin and tonic," she murmured, then turned to Teagan who looked pretty relaxed.

"What happened to your lady friend?" she asked with mild interest. "She seemed into you until she hurried off. Seems your game is a little off. Would you like some pointers?"

He chuckled—the sound tickling her vertebrae like fingers dancing down her spine—and said, "Pointers from you? Hmm…not sure."

"And why not?"

"Because I'm not really a catch-and-release kind of guy."

Heat crawled into Harper's cheeks, caught off guard by how easily Teagan seemed to laser in on her strategy, but she knew it was impossible for him to know. Whatever she was keying in on was her own paranoia. Harper graced Teagan with a small smile. "Why hold on to one, when there are so many to choose from?"

Teagan nodded as if ceding her point until he countered, saying, "Why continue to draw in fish you have no intention of keeping?"

"The thrill of the chase?" she suggested coyly as the bartended pushed her drink toward her. She rewarded him with a blinding smile and a modest tip.

"I don't see you chasing anyone," he pointed out, watching as she lifted the glass to her lips. "I see it the other way around. But something tells me, that's your game."

It was true. Harper rarely chased—she snared.

"Okay, Mr. Observant…what else do you see?"

The minute she threw the question out there, she knew it was a mistake. Teagan was sharp. There was something about him that cut through the haze and pushed away her carefully constructed web. He wasn't in a rush to fall all over her and that wasn't something she was accustomed to, either.

Teagan grinned, amused at her rash response. "You sure you want me to answer that?"

Actually, go ahead and forget I said it.

She graced him with a patronizing smile. "Darling, I can't wait to hear what you think you see after knowing me for a total of fifteen minutes."

Teagan swiveled on his chair to face her directly. She sucked in a tight breath as her heart rate quickened, but she held her smile. To her surprise, he reached for her hand and turned it over to observe her palm.

Was he psychic or something? Her smile turned wary. "What are you doing?"

"Shh…"

He lightly traced the faint lines in her palm, sending shivers rioting up her forearm.

"Am I going to be famous?" she teased, if only to quell the racing of her pulse at his touch. "Is this your schtick? Hey, baby, let me tell you your future?"

He graced her with a charming smile and released her hand.

"Well?"

Good God, she could still feel the heat of his fingertips sliding across her skin. Harper absently rubbed at her palm to stop the sensation.

"You, Harper Riley, are a man-eater."

"And what makes you say that?" she asked, trying to play off his observation as if humoring him.

"Because your hands are soft as a baby's behind, which means you rarely lift a finger to do much work. Your manicure is perfect, not a single hangnail in sight. Your hair is gorgeous, which means you take the time to have it styled regularly, and your body... Well, you and I both know your body is toned, taut and flawless, which tells me you take care of yourself religiously. Why else would a woman put so much effort into being perfect? Unless she was on the hunt. We men may be stupid but some clichés are true."

Harper scoffed at his assessment. "Or it could mean I have good genes and I like to work out because it feels good. Besides, who said I was perfect?"

"I'm not finished," he said, gesturing to her heels. "Expensive designer shoes, a dress that fits like it was made for you, diamond earrings and a Louis Vuitton bag that probably cost more than a small car. Now tell me you're not on the prowl."

He was not only right, he was shockingly eagle-eyed for a man.

Was he gay? "How do you know anything about women's clothing?" she asked. "Do you have a thing for expensive bags and shoes?"

He leaned in, his voice tickling her ear. "I've had a few girlfriends with expensive tastes...and I pay attention."

Danger, Harper, a voice whispered.

The last thing she needed was a man who knew how to pick up on subtle cues. What if he caught on to her plan with Stuart?

She couldn't afford to mess around. Harper needed that payday.

But their gazes locked as if tethered. Her will to cut the contact faltered in the pull of those gorgeous eyes. The man had won the genetic lottery. Handsome without being pretty, rugged without being ill-mannered. Yes, Teagan was dangerous, indeed.

"I think I'm going to call it a night," she announced, rising from her seat.

"You haven't finished your drink."

Finally breaking their gaze, Harper said, "I think I've had enough. Good night, Mr. Carmichael."

And then, with the effort it took to walk calmly from the room, Harper thought her heart might explode from her chest.

Only when she was safely in her room did she release the shaky breath caught in her lungs.

Teagan was everything she didn't want—so why had it been so hard to ignore him?

4

THAT WENT SMASHINGLY TERRIBLE, he mused with a wry twist of his lips.

Not only had he chased away two women, he was left with the crazy impulse to follow Harper to her room like a damn stalker.

Clearly she wasn't interested, right?

No, Teagan didn't buy that act. Harper was into him, but for some reason she didn't want to be.

He didn't like drama or baggage. Hell, he had enough of his own to bother with without dragging someone else's aboard.

So if Harper wanted to run, he wasn't about to chase her.

Sounded good in theory.

Sounded damn good.

Except, he was already formulating what he might say to her when he showed up at her door.

Maybe words were the problem. Maybe he ought to just kiss her senseless.

Harper looked as if she needed a little something in her life to muss up that perfectly styled hair.

She was gorgeous, no doubt about that, but he wanted to see her, no makeup, bed head, and in shorts and a T-shirt.

Preferably over breakfast.

That's the liquor talking, bud. Slow your roll.

Probably true.

He had just enough alcohol in his system to lower his inhibitions, but this whole thing was outside of his comfort zone.

Remember the good old days when you just hooked up with someone at the bar and if things worked out you started the dialogue?

Now he was on a singles cruise. If that didn't feel like geriatric dating, he didn't know what did.

He didn't have the same kind of luck as J.T., meeting the love of his life when she walked into the hangar to hire him.

Forget the part where she almost got them killed. *Hey, no one's perfect.*

And maybe if he wasn't in a bit of a drought, he wouldn't be fixating on Harper.

Yeah, that was it. It was the drought's fault.

For the past year and a half, his life had been consumed by Blue Yonder. Trying to keep the business afloat had been harder than either he or J.T. had anticipated.

You know it's bad when you have to choose between buying toilet paper or food because if you buy both, bills weren't going to get paid.

Hell, he'd even considered reenlisting.

Thankfully, J.T. had talked him out of that temporary insanity. He had no interest in the soldier life anymore. That was a young man's game.

And although J.T. liked to remind him that they were neither old nor unfit for duty, both Teagan and J.T. had become accustomed to the luxuries of civilian life.

So, about that drought.

Teagan tried to think of the last time he'd dated.

It took a minute—probably longer than it should have—but his last date had been disappointing. Not because she hadn't been hot, not because she hadn't had a great personality, just because his mind had been elsewhere.

Owning your own business had a tendency to suck the energy from every possible outlet.

Including his mojo.

The woman, Clara, had been more than willing to take it to the next level. But his conscience stopped him when things became heated.

Although in hindsight, telling a woman you have to go, after making out for a good solid hour, clothes nearly in a pile, was probably not the best.

But Teagan had known that if he had slept with her, it would have been worse.

Score one for a conscience; zero for his blue balls.

He ought to forget about Harper completely. The whole point of this cruise was to meet up with someone. Maybe he didn't have to find Mrs. Right, maybe she could just be Mrs. Right Now.

He wasn't above enjoying himself if the moment was right. But even as he scanned the room, looking for someone who might interest him for the evening, all he could think about was Harper, in her room.

Alone.

It was almost as if he didn't have a choice. His brain wasn't going to let anyone else upstairs. Perhaps if he went to Harper, got firmly rejected, he could get the closure he needed and move on.

Just as he was about to make good on his idea, the bar stool was occupied again, only this time, it was with one of the men who'd been clustered around Harper like a drone bee around the queen.

The man didn't waste time and got right to it. "Hello, friend, whatcha drinking?" he asked.

Curious, Teagan answered, "Beer."

"Ahh, down-to-earth man," he said, after ordering a glass of wine. "Look, I'm just going to get down to brass tacks because that's the kind of man I am, which I'm sure you can appreciate."

Teagan couldn't wait to see where this was going.

"You see, I'm the kind of man who sees what he wants and goes after it—no matter the obstacles. That's how I am in business and how I am in life."

"Good for you," Teagan replied, tipping back his beer.

"Yeah, so I think you'll understand what I mean when I say that I got dibs on the hot brunette."

Teagan made a point to peer around the room as if looking for said brunette. "Can you be more specific?"

"The one who was sitting right here a few minutes ago. Hot bod, long dark hair and a rack to die for. Ring a bell?"

Teagan didn't much like Harper being reduced to such simple attributes but what could he say? He'd been pretty much snagged by those very visual cues himself. Still...he didn't like when this douche did it.

"I'd say it's probably a good idea to let the lady decide who she wants to spend time with," Teagan said, finishing his beer. "Don't you think? I mean, she is an adult, capable of making her own decisions and something tells me, that Harper is the kind of woman who would take offense to hearing someone talk about her like you just did."

"You gonna tattle on me?" the man joked, but Teagan wasn't laughing. He was pretty much done with this conversation and the only thing keeping him from punching this guy's lights out was that he didn't want to be put in the brig. Or whatever served as a holding cell for unruly passengers. "So you're saying you're not going to back off?"

"Why would I do that?"

"Because I called dibs."

He called dibs. Good God, give me strength.

Teagan smirked as he rose from his seat. "Well, I'm not twelve and I don't recognize the dibs game any longer. She's not a piece of candy, she's a woman. If you can't interest her squarely on your own, then that's not my problem. Good luck with your *dibs*."

Teagan pushed past the man, leaving him to burn hot

coals into his back but Teagan didn't care. The man was an asshole.

But even so, the man had served one unexpected purpose— he'd given Teagan a much-needed splash of cold water on his overheated brain.

The purpose of this trip was to loosen up and have fun, not beat down every Tom, Dick and Harry who hoped to snag the "hot brunette with the smoking body," and if Mr. Swagger was any indication of what chasing after Harper Riley would be like, then Teagan was out.

As if the universe was listening, a sassy redhead cast a flirty smile his way and he responded in kind.

J.T. was a vocal proponent of redheads now.

And this one wasn't bringing gun-toting maniacs in her wake.

This trip may be salvageable, after all.

HER GAME FELT OFF. With Stuart being a no-show and then Teagan getting in her head, Harper felt tilted, which wasn't a good sign.

She needed to be on target to snag Stuart.

Harper changed into her pajamas, removed her makeup and then crawled into bed, phone in hand.

More research.

Stuart. Buck.

She stared at the most recent picture, taken at some toilet seminar where he'd been the lead speaker, and chewed her lip as she frowned.

The Toilet King.

Harper wrinkled her nose with distaste. That was a tall order, but Harper didn't care what other people said about her as long as the checks cleared.

Louis Vuitton bag.

Chanel dress.

Louboutin heels.

Teagan had been spot-on.

And the religious workouts—Pilates, CrossFit, Zumba, yoga—anything and everything to keep her body fit and toned.

It was exhausting.

She had no social life.

Friends were a luxury she couldn't afford.

And God only knew she never confided in her lovers about anything, because she wasn't the person they thought she was.

She played a part, for which she accepted payment in the form of expensive gifts and luxury vacations.

But she wouldn't be young forever.

Sooner or later, time would catch up to her and no amount of Pilates would keep her ass from succumbing to gravity.

Harper winced at the cruelty awaiting her and that fear renewed her purpose.

That's why Stuart was so important.

This one was going to marry her.

No more playing the mistress or girlfriend with nothing legally binding.

She couldn't live on gifts alone.

And that meant she had to be smart.

Stuart wasn't a stupid playboy with a trust fund.

He was a successful businessman who'd been loyal to his wife until the day she died.

Stuart held old-fashioned values and believed in hard work and fair play.

Honestly, Stuart was the kind of man Harper would have liked for a father or grandfather.

Except instead of going to Stuart for fatherly advice, she was going to seduce the man.

Harper groaned when a tiny bubble of bile rose in her throat.

What was wrong with her?

Stuart was not the worst she'd slept with.

He seemed kind, generous…and incredibly old.

Okay, maybe he wasn't the Crypt Keeper, but compared to Teagan, Stuart was a fossil.

She closed her eyes and immediately Teagan was there.

Hard muscles covering a solid, manly frame.

Sensual lips that played with a flirty smile and begged to be kissed.

How was a guy like Teagan single, anyway?

Either the women in his circles were incredibly stupid or he had some heinous defect.

Maybe he chewed his toenails.

Maybe he picked his nose and ate his boogers.

Or maybe he had some weird sexual fetish like armpit licking or he liked to dress up like a baby and be breast-fed.

Yes, keep thinking of Teagan as a deviant, a voice encouraged, *otherwise, you're going to find yourself pressed up against him before you know it.*

How long had it been since Harper had enjoyed a real relationship? Been with someone because she wanted to be, not because he was a target.

Just as she started to mourn her lack of true intimacy, the specter of the past rose to slap her.

It was hard to forget her mother's tears. The horrible sadness that clawed the personality out of Anna Riley, and Harper was sure that the subsequent drag on her immune system had eventually led to MS.

Whereas Anna had once been sweet, kind and way too trusting, time and repeated heartache had left the woman a shell.

The disease had robbed her of everything else.

Harper had been twelve when Rex had conned her mother out of their savings, leaving them with nothing but bad credit, crippling debt and no way out.

And her mom had gotten pregnant, too.

Harper blinked furiously at the unwanted tears that threatened to fall.

Some say that things happened for a reason.

Losing Rex's baby had been a blessing in disguise but it'd taken the final toll on Anna.

Harper's childhood had disintegrated, leaving behind nothing but cold, hard adulthood.

And she had vowed to never let a man do to her what had been done to Anna.

If anyone was going to suffer scars, it wouldn't be Harper from that moment forward.

She stilled for a moment to gather her focus.

That's it, remember the pain. Remember the reason men like Teagan are bad news.

Releasing a long breath, Harper felt a renewed sense of purpose and returned to her research.

Tomorrow…Stuart Buck.

5

VANESSA THOUGHT TO escape to her room, but when she was midway, she stopped. The point of this trip was to liberate herself from her past. To stop mourning a life she didn't miss.

Her and Dale's relationship had been complicated, like most romantic relationships. They'd married young, and although there were too many bad times to count, there were good times, too.

A lifetime together had seamed a jagged stitch but it had bound them just the same.

One kid.

A daughter.

She'd done her due diligence as a wife and mother. Sabrina was off living her life as she should, but it'd left Vanessa alone to deal with Dale and their shortcomings.

Just as things had become unbearable, Dale had done the honorable thing and died of a heart attack.

Boom. No flash and bang. No long, drawn-out illness… just gone.

Sometimes Vanessa still thought she could smell his Old Spice cologne.

As much as Dale had been an overbearing, pigheaded jerk at times, he'd also been her best friend.

What she'd thought was going to be a grand dating adventure after he'd passed, had turned into a sad realization that she'd never truly mourned the man who'd been her constant companion for thirty years.

And somehow that young cutie at the bar had managed to activate that button that she'd been trying to hide for a year.

Her best friend, Lola, said the best way to get over a man was to get under another.

So far that had only worked temporarily.

But since Vanessa didn't have any other advice to follow, she'd booked her first cruise, and followed it with another.

Right about now, she was thinking it all might've been a waste of money.

She didn't have the right mind-set to jump into another fling.

She wanted…something more.

So was it time to change her game plan? Look for something a little less transient? Maybe admit that Lola had been completely bonkers to suggest a series of one-night stands to heal her bleeding heart?

Vanessa found herself on the upper deck gazing at the stars. The balmy air kissed her cheek as the dark waves lapped at the side of the massive ship.

Being a cougar was fun for a time but stargazing alone was really unsatisfying.

"Oh, pardon me."

Vanessa startled at the apology and turned to see an older gentleman turning to leave her to her solitude but she stopped him. "It's okay," she said. "I don't mind a little company."

The man smiled and returned. "Are you certain? I don't want to intrude."

"Being alone isn't all it's cracked up to be."

He nodded. "Man is not meant to walk alone."

"Or woman," she added with a tiny chuckle. "Being with

someone is a hard habit to break when you've been married for thirty years."

"My wife passed a year ago," he said quietly. "She was my best friend. Sometimes I don't know what I'm doing without her."

Vanessa nodded, the tears threatening to return. She laughed ruefully. "Now, don't get the waterworks started or they'll never stop."

"Okay, I promise, no more talk of sad things. I'm not sure why I came out here. I thought about going to the meet and greet but changed my mind at the last minute. I couldn't bring myself to walk into the meat market."

"It does feel like that sometimes, doesn't it?"

He sighed. "Things are so different from when I was young. Dating was much more civilized. But listen to me, waxing nostalgic over times gone by. That's what old people do, right?"

The man's self-deprecating laugh was very soothing. There was something about him that relaxed Vanessa in a way she hadn't felt in a long time. "Are you here to meet your soul mate?" she teased lightly.

"I doubt fate would be so kind as to grace me with two soul mates but I'm open to meeting someone I can share my life with. How about you?"

Vanessa considered her answer for a moment. "I don't know if soul mates exist, honestly. I want to believe in the idea but I don't know… I'm just unsure if it's truly possible. But I'm envious of those who come close to having that."

"You were married to a terrible man?" he inquired with a frown.

"No, not really. He was just…Dale. Hardheaded, stubborn, pigheaded, my-way-or-the-highway kind of man. But he was a good provider," Vanessa added when it seemed all she could focus on were Dale's negative traits. "And a good father. I guess that's more than what some women get."

The man regarded her with a smile in his eyes and she

realized he had the kindest eyes she'd ever seen. "And your wife? What was she like?"

"She was smart, stubborn, sassy…all the things I like in a woman. She didn't take any garbage from anyone, least of all me. But she was also an amazing cook and homemaker. Anywhere with her in it was home."

Vanessa couldn't help but feel a little inadequate in light of the man's superwife, but it wasn't fair or attractive to put her insecurities on his memory so she simply smiled and murmured, "Sounds like you were a lucky man."

"I was," he agreed. "But it's easy to remember the good times when someone is gone, right? It wasn't always perfect, but it was good."

"Yeah," Vanessa agreed, realizing that was also true of her relationship with Dale. Grief had made her bitter and reckless, but she was finally coming out of that place. "It was good."

"Well, I think I'll turn in," he announced with a charming smile. "Thank you for the company."

Vanessa returned the smile and truly meant it when she said, "I hope you find your next soul mate."

"I wish the same for you."

And then he left, leaving her to the quiet, abandoned deck.

Vanessa exhaled and realized too late, she hadn't gotten his name.

Nor had she given hers.

TEAGAN AWOKE ALONE in his bed and for that he was very grateful.

Last night's details had gotten hazy after a few more drinks and, while he remembered dancing with a hot redhead, he didn't quite recall getting to his room.

His head ached and his mouth tasted as if a gnome had shit in it.

Rolling to his side, he rose from the bed and guzzled a

bottled water from the minifridge, then, with the final swallow, tossed back a few aspirin.

The best way he knew to work off a hangover was to sweat it out. Sliding on some workout gear and slipping on his tennis shoes, he made his way to the onboard gym.

J.T. had assured him that the gym on the ship was top-notch and that had been the saving grace. Military habits died hard and he couldn't start his day without getting his sweat on.

Also helped to keep the love handles at bay.

Teagan walked into the gym and grinned with approval. Yes, this was going to work.

The workout facility was bigger than most gyms in the city, with state-of-the-art equipment. Everything was shiny and clean, sanitized and ready for anything.

Surprisingly, it was nearly empty.

Guess not many people enjoyed working out when they were on vacation.

He made his way to an open treadmill and realized the woman punishing herself two treadmills over was none other than Harper.

She was pounding the track at a fast clip, earbuds firmly in her ears as she zoned out. Everything about Harper was toned and tight. His initial decision to steer clear of the drama-magnet evaporated the minute he saw her again.

He loved women who didn't play around at the gym. Harper was working up a sweat, hair tied in a messy ponytail, wearing simple, no-nonsense running shorts and sports bra.

She wasn't there to impress—she was there to work.

God, that was a turn-on.

Instead of choosing the treadmill closest to her, Teagan climbed on the original one he'd picked, looping his towel over the handle and putting his water in the holder.

His head was still pounding but he would just have to power through. Once he was in the zone, the pain would fade.

After about ten minutes, he upped the pace and started running at a good clip. It felt great to move with the pent-up tension bunching his muscles.

Maybe afterward he'd find the masseuse and really live it up with a good rubdown.

Before too long, he realized he and Harper were running at the same tempo. Their steps were synced even though neither had timed it purposefully. Harper would be a good running partner.

J.T. always bitched that Teagan was trying to leave him behind. J.T. preferred a more leisurely pace whereas Teagan liked to move.

Apparently, Harper liked to move, too.

He glanced over at the exact time that Harper did. Their eyes locked. Sweat trickling down their faces, arms and legs pumping. She'd been running longer than him and yet her pace was as strong.

Fatigue started to eat at his stamina but he didn't want to slow before her.

Harper dragged her gaze away and returned to her focal point, ignoring him.

But it was an act. If he could sense the energy between them, then she could, too.

Like it or not, they had something between them that wouldn't go away.

And while Teagan had never considered running some kind of aphrodisiac, he was fighting an inappropriate arousal as they ran in tandem.

He couldn't stop wondering how well they'd sync up if they were pressed skin against skin.

Working up a sweat in a different way.

Ah, hell. Now is not the time to get a stiff one.

As much as Teagan wanted to win this endurance race, he knew Harper had beat him.

Dialing down the pace, he caught a minute twitch of her lips and he could practically hear her crowing in victory.

Teagan smothered his laugh and, after a cooldown, moved to the weight machines.

Only this time, he purposefully selected a machine in Harper's direct eye line.

Clearly having won that round, Harper slowed her pace and started her cooldown.

But Teagan wanted to keep her heated.

Pushing the weight bar overhead, he started his reps, knowing full well that his muscles were glistening and swelling as he worked.

He bit back his own victory crow when she couldn't keep her focus. Her gaze kept darting to his arms and away again, as if she couldn't quite help herself from taking a peek even though she didn't want to.

Yeah, she could try and deny the attraction all she wanted.

Proof is in the pudding, darlin'.

Finished her workout, Harper wiped her face and stepped off the treadmill, risking a glance at Teagan one last time before she left the gym, practically running away in her haste.

He chuckled. Maybe the chase was worth the aggravation he would encounter.

Harper was fast becoming his favorite part about this trip.

Now, the question was…how did he get Harper to feel the same about him?

6

HARPER WIPED THE sweat from her face and hurried to her room to shower.

Her pulse raced even as she closed her door and stripped.

The nerve of that guy, to insert himself into her workout.

As if all that sweaty muscle would impress her.

Like she'd never seen a well-built male.

Harper barked a short laugh as if that alone would bolster her argument with herself.

But she was still shaking.

Her fingers were trembling and her insides felt twisted into knots.

She had too much restless energy and no outlet.

Get in the shower, start the day, just as you would have if Teagan hadn't shown up.

Sound advice.

Eventually, she'd settle down and everything would go back to normal.

Harper turned on the water and stepped into the spray, gasping when the cold water hit her skin.

Yesss! A cold shower was exactly what she needed to cool down.

Why was Teagan so… She didn't have the word for what Teagan was.

A *distraction*, that's what he was.

She closed her eyes and drifted into the spray, letting the water pelt some sense into her head.

But Teagan was right there in her thoughts, refusing to leave.

That smile, that dimple. What was a grown-ass adult doing with a dimple in his cheek, anyway?

Dimples were for boy bands and babies.

Except there was nothing boyish about Teagan.

She groaned. All that hard, firm flesh…her fingers itched to touch.

Stop it.

Just stop.

She was tangled in knots, her thoughts couldn't travel a straight line. It was the backup of sexual energy that had nowhere to go.

Harper looked at the showerhead and a thought came to her.

It'd been a fleeting spark of a thought but once it caught, a fire followed.

Leaning against the wall, she placed her foot on the tiny ledge that masqueraded as a seat and brought down the showerhead from its cradle. The water pressure was strong enough but not too strong.

Dare she say, just right?

Only one way to find out.

Closing her eyes, Harper brought the showerhead to her aching sex, nestling the pulsating jets against the swollen and ready nub between her folds.

Immediate pleasure flushed through her body as awareness flooded her senses. Harper gasped as she adjusted position, allowing for a better pulse, and squeezed her eyes shut when the violent threat of an immediate orgasm nearly stole the strength from her legs.

She was so close. Tantalizing close.

But she didn't want to come just yet.

Harper wanted to savor the sweetness a little bit more. Teagan.

His name floated from her thoughts and escaped through her parted lips as the pleasure mounted.

She ground the pulsing jets against her harder, relishing the pressure as her body began to shake.

Her thoughts were unruly, going unerringly straight to Teagan. Imagining what it would feel like to be pressed against him, his tongue inside her mouth, demanding everything from her, pushing her ever closer to that beautiful shattering moment.

Oh, God. She gasped, her free hand gripping the side of the shower as her knees wobbled.

Teagan...yesss!

Harper came hard. So hard that her toes curled into tight buds as her muscles clenched so violently that she might never wear heels again.

But it was worth it.

Dropping the showerhead from nerveless fingers, she sank to the floor, breathing hard.

The spray swung wildly and smacked her in the face, sending a wash of water straight up her nose as she struggled to get it under control.

Coughing, she rose on unsteady feet and replaced the showerhead in its cradle.

She'd made herself stupid with that orgasm.

Just *thinking* about Teagan had made her come.

So what would happen if she actually found herself skin to skin with the gorgeous man?

She might just spontaneously combust.

Harper chuckled weakly at her own joke and exhaled a long breath.

Well, at least she was relaxed now.

She eyed the showerhead as if it were a conspirator and said, "This is between me and you. No one else needs to know. Got it?"

Of course, the showerhead said nothing.

But somehow Harper felt better just saying the words out loud if only to pound the sentiment home to her stubborn subconscious.

She didn't want Teagan.

She wanted…what was his name? Oh, that's right, Teagan…no!

Stuart.

Stuart Money Bucks.

Think of those lovely millions and all the lovely ways you are going to spend it, she reminded herself, lathering up the body wash. So what if Stuart was old enough to be her grandfather and Teagan looked like sex on a stick. Money was the great equalizer.

That's all she needed to remember.

THE ITINERARY FOR today was relaxed. A full day at sea as the *Nautica* sliced through the waters toward Mexico. There were a number of activities on the schedule if you were so inclined but mostly it was about relaxation and fun.

There were casinos and restaurants, spas, shopping and more food.

So much food! If Teagan came back with love handles, despite punishing himself at the gym, J.T. would never let him live it down.

His cell rang and he saw—speak of the devil—J.T. was calling.

"Hey," Teagan answered. "You know this is going to cost me an arm and a leg."

"I told you to get the international plan but you didn't want to spring for the temporary cost. That's on you."

"I didn't think I was going to get a check-up call from my little brother," he returned drily. "What's up?"

"Just wondering how the trip is going. You know, seeing if my money was well spent."

"Next time you want to blow money, just give me the cash."

"That good, huh?"

"It's not bad, just not really my scene."

"Teagan, you've been out of the scene so long I doubt you'd remember what your scene looks like," J.T. joked. Teagan had to admit his little brother was right, but he wasn't going to give him the satisfaction of admitting it out loud. "Look, you're being a good sport about it, so have some fun. Be a tourist. Buy funny hats and drink too many margaritas. Make some memories you can regret later. Every old man needs some questionable life choices to reminisce about in the old folks home, so get to it."

"I can always borrow a few of yours," Teagan reminded his brother. "I think you made enough bad choices to last us both a lifetime."

"Hey, not all bad choices turn out to be bad in the end. We're getting a new plane and revitalizing our business from my last bad decision and I happen to sleep next to the most beautiful woman in the world because of it. So, in the end, my choice wasn't bad at all."

"You're burning dollars with your philosophical bullshit," Teagan said, rolling his eyes. "Was there anything else you needed to tell me? Any news on the plane delivery?"

"Yeah, been pushed back a few weeks. So really there's nothing stopping you from letting your hair down and going crazy. I got things here."

Teagan grunted an answer and said his goodbye. Then he turned his phone off. He didn't want any more calls from his little brother.

Knowing J.T., the little shit was probably purposefully calling him just to jack up the phone bill. Brothers were funny that way.

Teagan knew he could trust J.T. to hold down the fort, but it wasn't exactly in his nature to hand over the keys to the castle while he rode off into the sunset for a while.

That'd always been J.T.'s MO.

But maybe J.T. had a small point.

Hell, the money was spent already.

Maybe he ought to go buck wild and just whoop it up.

Maybe he ought to make it his mission to catch the lovely Harper Riley.

An instant smile threatened even as he thought of her.

Yeah, that could make the trip bearable.

Teagan spent his adult life making sure that J.T. stayed out of trouble. Maybe it was his turn to do something reckless.

Harper was playing it cool.

Guess it was time to turn up the heat.

Oh, Harper, you're about to experience a little Carmichael charm.

He gave the mirror a cheesy grin and wagged his eyebrows.

Okay, so he was a little rusty.

Let's start with the basics.

Teagan wrapped the towel around his midsection and flexed, popping out the muscles in his abs and pecs.

Respectable, he noted with pride.

Damn respectable.

He flexed a little more, some poses nonchalant, others obvious.

Then, because all men were essentially kids at heart, he whipped off his towel and swiveled his hips so that his cock started to sway.

Ding dong, baby.

He did that a few times until it started to become painful.

Okay, that's enough, his inner adult chastised and he returned the towel to his hips.

He knew Harper was attracted to him physically, but she resisted him anyway. So it had to be a mental game.

He had to interest Harper on a different level if he wanted her guard to come down.

So it was time to figure out just what made Harper tick. Time for a little recon.

7

HARPER SMOOTHED HER hair and pulled it off to the side so the dark curls draped over her shoulder, then placed her wide-brimmed hat on her head. A final look in the mirror confirmed she looked casually well put together, yet refined at the same time. Stuart wasn't going to be wowed by a woman who seemed classless. If Harper wanted a ring on her finger, she had to play things right.

Exiting her room, she accidentally bit her tongue as Teagan's door opened and there he was in all his muscled, hot-bodied glory.

Of all the terrible timing.

And wearing a shirt that molded to his biceps as if it was painted on. Like anyone needed to see that!

Well, she didn't.

She had no interest whatsoever in running her tongue down that ridged stomach to find what lay at the end of his happy trail.

Nope. Not at all.

Sure you don't.

So she certainly didn't want a quick reminder of how Teagan had unwittingly helped her to "relax" in the shower.

Her cheeks flared with heat but she managed a brief smile, betraying nothing.

"Did you enjoy yourself last night?" she asked as they began to walk to the elevator. "Close any deals?"

Teagan laughed and shook his head as if he wasn't one to share secrets and said, "How about you? Did you sleep alone?"

"A lady never shares such tawdry details," she returned with a coy look. Let him think that she'd been doing anything aside from sitting in her pajamas, doing what was the equivalent of homework. "Well, at any rate, I doubt you'll be lonely this trip. You have that look some women find appealing."

"Some?"

"Well, you can't be everyone's cup of tea. It doesn't work that way," she said, laughing at the sudden arch of his brow. "My, someone's ego is quite healthy, isn't it?"

"Haven't had many complaints," he said, pushing the elevator button. "So what's on your agenda today? Shopping?"

"I might check out some of the shops. I do love boutiques." Total lie. She hated shopping. It also felt like homework. To be honest, she was much more comfortable with her hair in a bun, watching a movie in her yoga pants than being all dressed up. "And you? What's on your plan?"

"I think I might check out the giant slide."

Harper laughed as if that were an absurd idea but secretly she wished she could do the same. She'd seen the slide and been instantly wowed by how fun it must be to zip down that slippery thing. But it wasn't as if she was about to do it. "Well, have fun," she said, stepping into the elevator.

"I will," he said, following.

The awkward ensuing silence did nothing to quell the jittery flutter in her stomach. Why were elevators so small? She could barely breathe.

And whatever cologne he was wearing…it was…heavenly.

But she wasn't about to say that. Harper rubbed her nose

with a delicate sniff. "My goodness, whatever you're wearing is activating my sinuses."

"Hmm…nothing but my skin, darlin'."

He smelled like that naturally?

Good Lord.

The doors opened and they both exited, going in separate directions.

The fact that Teagan so easily left her in the dust gave her pause. Had she misread the signals? She thought for sure he was into her. Not that it mattered. But maybe her ego was a little bruised because he'd so easily brushed her off.

Did she want him to chase her just so she could turn him down?

Maybe a little.

Deliberately shoving any thought of Teagan far from her mind, Harper prepared to put Phase One into effect. Stuart was supposed to be on the upper deck, enjoying breakfast—his usual poached eggs and dry toast—and so that's where she was heading, too.

She'd paid handsomely to be seated with Stuart, which, with enough careful flirting, should open the door to more private time together.

Ah! Right as rain. The man was nothing if not habitual. Stuart, his bald head covered with a jaunty hat—that was oddly endearing on him, but on anyone else would've looked like a flat pancake perched on his dome—was enjoying his eggs, chatting with the others at his table.

Harper made a point of pretending to look for her table and then approached the open seat with a small smile. "I believe I'm seated with you," she said, and Stuart immediately rose to pull out her chair like a gentleman. Murmuring a "Thank you," she slid into the seat and nodded a hello to the others, as well. She made a show of noticing Stuart's eggs and asked, "How are the eggs? Done properly? I do so enjoy a perfectly poached egg."

"Very good," Stuart answered with a gleam in his eye

as if he appreciated someone who also enjoyed his particular tastes. As expected, Stuart introduced himself. "Stuart Buck, pleasure to make your acquaintance." He gestured around the table. "This is Marv, Genevieve, Stella and Patrick."

"The pleasure is all mine," Harper said, allowing Stuart to press a gallant kiss to the back of her hand. "Harper Riley."

"Harper, may I order you a plate?" he asked solicitously, and Harper nodded with a smile.

"That would be lovely," she said, playing the part of the demure lady for his benefit. Stuart was old-fashioned to his core. It was sweet in a way, but she needed to stop looking at him as a "sweet" man and start seeing him as a potential lover.

Ugh. Why is this so hard?

The waiter appeared and Stuart placed her order. He returned to Harper, interest in his eyes. "You are a lovely young lady," he remarked and the rest of the table concurred. They were all middle-aged or older. In comparison, she looked like she could be their granddaughter, or daughter at the very least. "And you are not attached?"

"I could say the same for you," she teased, turning the tables. "How is it that a handsome, stylish devil such as yourself is not already taken?"

Stuart chuckled and said, "Well, my beloved wife is recently deceased and I'm still acclimating to the single life, but to be honest, it's not really my style. I don't think I was cut out for the bachelor life."

Marv agreed with a hearty laugh. "I hear ya, Stewie. I'm happiest with a nice, soft woman cuddled up beside me. It's just not the same without a female around the house to make it a home."

Harper wanted to be offended for Stuart for that atrocious familiarity but he took it in stride. He seemed to really enjoy hanging out with the eclectic group. Maybe it was true that

Stuart did seek out the company of those in the trenches rather than those in his own tax bracket.

If so, that was a point in Stuart's favor. One of the most exhausting aspects of her "job" was putting on a front for all those stuffy rich bastards she had to circulate around to find her next meal ticket.

"So what do you do for a living?" she asked, trying to strike up a harmless conversation. "Let me guess...retired and living the single life in Boca Raton."

"Not retired, but I don't punch a clock, either," Stuart answered, being a bit vague. She didn't blame him. If she were a gazillionaire, she wouldn't advertise, either.

"Sounds like a good setup." She turned to one of the women. "How about you, Stella?"

"Retired teacher," Stella answered with a good-natured grin on her round face. She had apple cheeks that reminded Harper of a grandmother in a fairy tale. "I taught primary grades for thirty years. Best time of my life, but I'm ready to travel and do things for me for a change."

"How sweet," Harper murmured. "Good teachers are so hard to come by these days." She looked around the table. "Any children?"

Stella and Patrick shook their head no, but Stuart and Genevieve both answered in the affirmative.

Marv piped in saying, "Not yet but I'm always willing to try! I figure I still have time, right?" He poked Patrick in the side and guffawed. Marv was like a used car salesman who laughed at his own jokes. He was goofy and loud but the table seemed to tolerate him well enough. "I'm still spry enough to get the job done, I can assure you that!"

The table chuckled and Harper paused as the waiter returned with her food, placing the plate before her. "Smells wonderful," she said for Stuart's benefit. Harper wasn't actually a huge fan of eggs, but she made a show of digging in. The first bite, she nodded with fake pleasure, confirming his assessment of the eggs. "Yes, very good."

Small talk followed as they enjoyed breakfast but Harper was only half-invested. Somehow, her gaze found Teagan as he sat at his table next to a voluptuous blonde who immediately attached herself to his side.

What happened to going on the big slide? Obviously, he'd changed his mind.

She tried not to care what Teagan was doing or with whom, but even as Harper repeatedly refocused, smiling and flirting on autopilot, she was preoccupied with what Teagan was doing with the blonde.

Somehow, Teagan and Harper locked gazes from across the room and Harper's breath actually hitched in her chest. It was like staring into the sun.

He did something to her insides that she couldn't quite quell.

Turning to Stuart, she blinded him with her best smile. "I was thinking of walking off some of this breakfast. Would you mind keeping me company?"

"I'd be delighted," he said, rising and pulling her chair out for her. He winked at the table in good humor. "Only a fool would decline an offer from such a lovely young lady."

"Stewie, you lucky dog," Marv called out with another loud chuckle. "Don't do anything I wouldn't do."

Harper was happy to leave the table—and Teagan—behind.

Phase One was going as planned.

WATCHING HARPER IN action was like watching a fox out-maneuver the mouse.

The old guy being the mouse.

Damn, he swore privately, disappointed. Harper had her eye on the older man. As in, a much older man.

Was she into old guys? Or was there something else?

Only one way to find out.

Teagan returned his attention to the cute blonde, Erin, sitting next to him, doing her best to snag his interest by leaning in to give him a nice view of her cleavage. He smiled and said, "You seem the kind of person who knows what's happening." Appealing to her ego. When she responded with a giggly grin, he knew he had her. "What can you tell me about that older gentleman leaving with the brunette."

Teagan gestured discreetly and Erin followed his lead. She returned to him, her eyes bright with the thrill of sharing gossip. "I don't know the brunette, but the old guy is known as The Toilet King."

"Toilet King?" he repeated. "Because…?"

"Not because he's weird in the sack or anything, you naughty thing," she tittered, playfully slapping him on the arm and lingering a little longer than necessary on his bicep. "He made his money off some toilet gadget. So that's why he's called The Toilet King."

"Married and looking for a mistress, or single and looking for a wife?"

Erin shrugged. "I don't know about that. All I know is that he's a real gentleman. Always pushing in a lady's chair and being very…what's the word…"

"Chivalrous," he supplied helpfully.

Erin snapped her fingers and bobbed her head. "Yep. That's it. He's real old-school. It's kinda sweet, actually. But I don't know why he came onto this boat when he could have a yacht all to himself. If I had the money, I wouldn't step foot on something so basic as a cruise ship."

Teagan made a show of glancing around. "I don't know, this rig seems pretty fancy. It's even got a slide."

She giggled again. "You're adorable. What are you doing for the rest of the day?"

"I was thinking of trying out that slide. Want to come?"

"I'd go anywhere with you, handsome, however," she added coyly, "I can think of other ways to get wet that are far more fun."

"I can only imagine," he said with a smile. "But I've got my eye on that slide right now."

"In that case, I'll pass on the slide but I hope you'll take a rain check on my offer."

Teagan watched Erin leave the breakfast deck and he questioned his sanity.

Erin wasn't hard on the eyes—hell, those breasts were practically a crime—but he wasn't interested in a quick wick dip.

But now that he had a clearer picture of what Harper was up to, he was quickly warming to the idea of messing with her game.

So, the reason Harper was cozying up to the old man was money.

No two ways to pretty that up.

Harper was a gold digger.

Thoughts already buzzing elsewhere, he headed for his room.

Vanessa, the hot cougar who'd left on uncertain terms the other night, was exiting her room. Uncertainty slowed his step—she had looked ready to cry last night when she bailed—and he wasn't sure if they were still on good terms.

But surprisingly, Vanessa had nothing but smiles for him. "Don't you look fresh as a daisy today," she said, appreciating his body as openly as before. "You are a tall drink of water and I'm so incredibly thirsty."

He uttered a nervous laugh and asked, "Are we okay? I feel really bad about how things ended between us. I never meant to bring up bad memories for you."

"Oh, honey, it wasn't you. I've got my own demons to slay. Sorry you got caught in the cross fire. Look, I know I'm not your type, so no hard feelings, but I do enjoy looking."

Relieved he hadn't ruined a potential friendship, he assured her, "You can look all you want." Then had the bright idea of inviting her along. "Hey, I was just about to check out that slide. Want to come?"

"That sounds like more fun than what I had planned, which was to peruse the ship stores to buy more things I don't need," she answered with self-deprecating humor. "Let me get my suit. Give me five minutes?"

"You got it," he said, grinning before disappearing to change, as well.

For the right person, Vanessa was going to be a catch. Teagan would have to keep an eye out for someone who might snag her eye.

It was the least he could do.

8

MAYBE HE WAS getting too old for these excursions, but his heart just wasn't into this cruise. Stuart enjoyed the energy of people, loved how he always seemed to meet someone interesting, but he was beginning to think that finding another love like his Rachel was unlikely.

Perhaps he was being greedy.

One great love in a lifetime was more than some received.

Lately, he'd become far more reflective than usual. He needed to shake things up—breathe life into the empty shell he was quickly becoming—because he was well aware that the sand in his hourglass was quickly slipping through that tiny hole.

Not that he was trying to be maudlin or anything, but the realization that you weren't immortal was a sobering one.

He wanted to spend his final years with someone he could laugh with, enjoy more than carnal pleasures with, see the world and soak up the adventures he had left to him with.

His secretary had secured him a full activity list but as he perused the itinerary, he just wanted to chuck it into the ocean.

He didn't want to live by lists any longer.

Board meetings.

Suck-up executives.

Gold-digging women.

He was tired of it all.

Was there no one in this world who was simply happy to be alive?

Stuart took a final look at the paper and purposefully crumpled it. No more itinerary. He was going to go wherever he fancied. Maybe he would just sit in the lounge or the upper deck and people watch.

But as he walked onto the bright sunlit deck, the delighted squeals of people overhead drew his attention. The slide. A slow smile found his mouth. Damn, he hadn't enjoyed something so reckless in a long time.

His doctor would say, "Don't even think about it," but the young man who still lived inside his old body was saying, "Hell yes, let's go!"

Stuart picked up the pace and felt lighthearted for the first time in a while. This was what his life was missing: good old-fashioned fun.

If he had a heart attack on the way down, well, hell, he'd enjoyed a good life, and the National Cancer Society was going to rejoice in the big sum of money he'd written to them in his will.

Life was for the living, right?

So let's get to living.

ONE THING WAS for sure—the view was amaze-balls.

The deep blue sea stretched endlessly as the liner churned through the water at a leisurely pace. The skies matched the blue of the water and the salty breeze was invigorating.

If nothing else, he'd have to thank J.T. for this view because, yeah, it was pretty awe-inspiring.

The giant slide curved in loops and long straightaways, encircling the ship before dumping them into a deep pool.

"You ready for this?" Teagan teased Vanessa as they climbed the stairs to the entrance. "You can still back out."

"You can back out if you want. I won't think any less of you," Vanessa returned, her eyes sparkling with the adventure. "I've always wanted to do this, but my husband wasn't a fan, so I missed out on all the things I would've done."

"Such as?"

"Zip lining in Bali, river rafting down the Colorado, horseback riding in Yosemite…so many things," she answered wistfully before adding with a bright smile, "But not anymore. I'm going to do whatever I want from now on. Want to come with me?"

He laughed at her persistence. "You're too much woman for me, Vanessa. I would never be able to keep up and then I'd have to turn in my man card."

She laughed. "Oh, honey, I won't tell if you won't."

He liked the easy banter with the older woman.

Suddenly, something caught Vanessa's eye. "Look at that. My friend from the upper deck." Vanessa gestured and Teagan saw none other than Stuart Buck, the man Harper had her eye on.

"You know him?" he asked.

"Oh, no, we just talked a little. He seems like a good guy. Very handsome, too."

Yes, indeed.

A thought began to germinate. Teagan had never professed to be a matchmaker, but he was staring at low-hanging fruit. Vanessa was a hot tamale of a woman and Stuart looked as if he could use a dose of spice in his life. And if Stuart was busy with Vanessa, that would certainly put a wrinkle in Harper's game, which pleased him more than it should.

Underhanded?

No more so than what Harper was doing chasing the old man.

And you know, he felt zero guilt.

None.

Zilch.

Someone had to look out for the guy. And that someone was going to be Teagan.

"He looks like he could use a friend," Teagan suggested. "Go ahead and tell him to come up with us."

"Are you sure?" Vanessa asked, but she was clearly pleased with his offer.

"Why not?" Teagan shrugged. "He doesn't seem to be here with anyone. What's the harm?"

Vanessa was definitely open to the idea but she hesitated just the same. "Goodness, I don't even know his name. He could be an ax murderer or something."

"I have it on good authority, ax murderers were excluded from this particular cruise," Teagan answered. "I think you're good."

"You don't think it's weird for me to just wave him down?"

"Naw. I can't imagine anyone who could show him what fun looks like more than you."

Vanessa's eyes sparkled at his flattery. "You are a silver-tongued devil but I love it. You're right, I'll just ask him and see what he says. All he can say is no, right?"

"That's the spirit."

"Stop being so damn adorable," she told him as she walked away.

Vanessa returned with Stuart in tow, already making introductions. "This is my friend Teagan. He's the sweetheart who suggested we grab you and bring you up with us."

"Thank you," Stuart said with a good-natured smile. "Nice to meet you." Then he turned to Vanessa and said, "You know, it dawned on me that we never actually introduced ourselves last night. I'm Stuart Buck."

"Vanessa Vermuelen," she replied with a mild blush and a covert glance Teagan's way. "Very nice to meet you."

"The pleasure is mine, I assure you."

Oh, this is already playing out perfectly.

Teagan grinned. "Man to man, I ought to warn you, Stuart, Vanessa is addictive. She's too much fun for one person to handle."

Stuart smiled with interest, the expression on his face both charming and intrigued—*damn, Stuart has skills*—and said, "That's where experience comes in handy, young man. Experience and wisdom."

"I don't know," Vanessa played along. "I'm not sure if you're up to this challenge. I'm in my sexual prime, if you know what I mean, and I have a voracious appetite."

Stuart's laughter reached his eyes. "Duly noted. If my ticker can handle this slide, I think I can handle just about anything. Shall we?" He gestured and Vanessa giggled as she stepped up to the tube.

"Want to go together?" Vanessa asked, and Stuart didn't need to be asked twice.

Except, being the gentleman, he turned to Teagan first. "Do you mind if I steal your girl?"

"Only if you promise to show her a good time," Teagan warned playfully. Stuart grinned and maneuvered himself behind Vanessa, gingerly clasping around her waist, hugging the curvy woman to his chest.

"Three...two...one..."

Whooosh!

They were down the slick tube of water, squealing like schoolkids. Vanessa's echoing laughter faded as they disappeared.

Teagan grinned, feeling pretty good about his intervention. He didn't know Vanessa at all but there was something about her that he just liked.

But now that Vanessa was busy with Stuart, he was going to find Harper.

Maybe he could persuade her to go on a ride down the tube, too.

The waterslide tube, of course.

9

HARPER FROWNED.

Today had not gone as planned.

Everything had been played to perfection at first. Stuart had taken the bait and they'd strolled around the shops.

Idle small talk.

Subtle flirting.

Shy smiles.

Just when Harper had been sure that a dinner invitation was forthcoming, Stuart politely excused himself with a *You're delightful company but I'll leave you to your shopping* and left.

Had she lost her touch?

What a horrifying thought.

No. It couldn't be that.

Maybe Stuart had digestive issues.

Blech.

Or maybe he…was interested in someone else?

Impossible.

Harper chewed her bottom lip, deep in worrisome thought. This could not be happening.

Men fell over themselves for her.

Especially older men.

She had alternate targets if Stuart fell through, but they weren't nearly as palatable as the kindly billionaire.

There was George Nealon—a short, bald, peacock of a man who liked his arm candy young and stupid, and playing that part would be excruciating.

There was Josef Levenson—tall, gangly, thick mustache and a stern expression permanently etched on his face. Intellectually, she would have to step up her game but he was worth the added effort.

Or, there was always Paul Delaque, a French businessman who had flirted with her endlessly when she'd been with someone else in common circles. Paul was easy on the eyes but light in the pocketbook and she'd rather not waste her time on a small fish.

No, it was too early to admit defeat. She just had to find the right bait.

Perhaps Stuart needed to remember that he was a hot-blooded man, still able to appreciate a fine woman on his arm.

Harper found herself in one of the upscale boutiques, considering a white skintight dress when a voice behind her said, "I don't know, that seems a little desperate."

Harper turned to find Teagan lounging against one of the displays, a subtle teasing grin on his rugged face. "Desperate?" she repeated, raising her brow. "Do tell."

Teagan pushed off to gently take the dress and replace it on the rack. "Catching a man's attention isn't that hard, but if you're looking to catch the right attention, you have to stop looking so thirsty."

Her heartbeat fluttered but she managed a cool smile. "I'm all ears."

Teagan selected a pretty sundress and held it up to her, nodding with approval. "Yes. This right here. Paired with cute sandals, hair in a ponytail, no makeup, this says to me, this girl knows how to enjoy life and I want to meet her."

Sounded like bliss. She couldn't remember the last time she didn't have to spend two hours getting ready.

Makeup contouring, facials to keep her skin fresh, Botox for those tiny, faint lines beginning to crease her brow, waxing and massage to keep her skin supple and soft.

In a word: exhausting.

But rich men didn't want the girl next door.

They wanted the walking waxed vagina with the bleached asshole, someone who dressed up their arm and made their lives seem so enviable.

They wanted a sex kitten, and sometimes they wanted everyone to know that they had ownership over the woman most men would give their left nut to touch.

Harper cast Teagan a patronizing look and returned to the original dress. She didn't know why she was playing with fire but it felt sinfully good to dabble. "You can't tell much from the rack. It's always good to try it on before making judgments."

"If you insist, but I think my opinion will stand."

"We'll see." With a saucy smile, she disappeared into the changing room and shimmied into the tight dress.

It was club wear—meant to draw attention to a woman's most obvious assets—tits and ass.

And damn, it was almost obscene.

She knew right away, a dress like this wouldn't appeal to Stuart, but she wanted to see Teagan's reaction when she emerged.

We'll see who seems desperate.

Fluffing her hair, Harper emerged from the dressing room and modeled the dress for Teagan.

His expression was worth framing.

He didn't try to hide his amazement. If his jaw could've dropped farther, it would've landed on the floor.

Teagan's gaze clouded with desire and Harper knew she had him by the short hairs.

This was more fun than she'd anticipated.

Harper did a small turn, stopping with a coy smile thrown over her shoulder and she thought the poor man might swallow his tongue. "Still seem desperate?" she teased.

As if remembering his original statement, Teagan swallowed and shrugged, finally finding his voice. "Well, it's beautiful for sure. I mean, you know you're hot. But I think sexy is also leaving something to the imagination."

"Are you saying I'm not sexy?"

"You know that's not what I meant. But shouldn't you make a man work for what he wants? If you put everything out there, what is there to chase after?"

Harper didn't have the luxury of being the coy, demure, hard-to-get woman.

She was her mother's sole support and her savings would not fund both her lifestyle and her mother's care.

But, Harper couldn't lie—she was enjoying Teagan's banter, even if she was dipping her toe in choppy waters.

"Let's put your theory to the test. You pick out the dress and I will see which one looks better."

Teagan smiled and immediately returned to the sundress, handing it to her. "Deal."

Harper smiled and took the dress into the dressing room. Getting out of the other dress was a challenge as it had molded to her skin, and once it was off, she breathed a private sigh of relief. She wouldn't admit it, but the sundress looked far more comfortable.

But Harper was proving a point. Not looking for comfort.

She exited the dressing room and modeled the sundress.

If Teagan had thought the slinky dress was sexy, he nearly lost his composure when she stepped out in the sundress.

Harper thrilled at the unspoken compliment. Cocking one brow, she asked, "Well? What's the verdict?"

"If I saw you from across a crowded room, wearing that dress, looking like you do right now, nothing would stand in my way from getting to know you."

The honesty in his answer stole her ability to breathe for a moment. Teagan wasn't playing a game. Unlike her, he was shooting straight from the hip.

Damn, she liked that about him.

She liked a lot of things about him.

Which was why, if she were smart, she'd return the dress, thank him for his opinion and leave him behind.

But Harper didn't want to do that.

She wanted to get to know Teagan better. What made those dimples pop out? Was he ticklish? What pissed him off? All those small, intimate details that were reserved for those who knew someone best… Harper wanted access.

What was it about Teagan that wiggled past her defenses and left her vulnerable to his charm?

"And if you saw me from across the room, what would you say to me?"

Teagan slowly stepped toward her as he closed the gap between them. The air around them crackled with sexual tension.

"Well, that's easy," he answered with a slow grin. "First, I'd say where have you been all my life and, second, I'd say cancel all your plans because you're spending the day with me."

A primal shock coursed through her and her heartbeat fluttered like a caged butterfly. Had anyone ever said anything so remotely sexy to her? "And what makes you think I would change all my plans for you? Maybe I was meeting someone."

"Maybe."

But what he didn't say was that it wouldn't matter. Harper knew that if that scenario had ever played out, she probably would have canceled her plans because the way he was looking at her right now was addicting.

"Well, maybe I'll go with this dress, after all."

Teagan smiled. "If you ever need a shopping buddy, I'd be happy to help you out."

She laughed. "Not many men would enjoy a full day of shopping. Is there something I should know about you?"

"Are you asking if I like to wear women's clothing at night when no one is watching? Well, who doesn't?" He teased. Then he said, "Just kidding. No, I have no interest in tripping around in high heels, but only a fool would turn down any opportunity to spend time with you."

Smooth talker.

Danger. Danger. Danger.

Harper bit her lip trying to hold back her delighted smile. *Men lie to get what they want*, a voice reminded her. *Remember all the promises and flattery Rex heaped on Mom when he first started coming around?*

Yeah, all lies.

The reminder cooled her jets. She wouldn't say that Teagan was anything like Rex at first glance. But what did she know about the man? The superficial story of the charming pilot wasn't enough.

"So you own a business?" she prompted. "Is it successful?"

"Sometimes."

She frowned. "What does that mean?"

"It means sometimes it's successful and sometimes it's not."

She didn't like that answer. "Most people want their business to be a success all of the time."

"Yes, and some people want to win the lottery. Doesn't always happen. But I love what I do and the way I look at it is if you have to work, you should work at something you love. That's a success story in my book."

"Not everyone has that luxury."

"Depends on the lifestyle you're trying to maintain. I have simple needs. As long as I can pay my bills, I'm good."

No, that wasn't enough for Harper. "Maybe with a little ambition, you could go from *sometimes* successful to *always* successful."

Why was she getting angry? It didn't matter how Teagan ran his business. He could do as he pleased. Whether he wanted to run his business into the ground or live check to check was none of her concern. Harper didn't want to have anything to do with that.

"As fun as this has been, I have to get going."

"Hot date?"

"I hope so."

"What time should I swing by your room to pick you up?"

Teagan's cheeky nerve both astounded and impressed her. "I don't recall making a date with you."

He grinned. "Sure you do. You even picked out a dress just for me."

And then before she could stop him, Teagan had given his credit card to the cashier, effectively paying for the purchase.

"See you at six, darlin'."

Harper watched as Teagan strolled out of the boutique as if he'd just won the lottery.

Damn, the man had style.

Even if her dress had just put a serious dent in his credit limit.

IF TIME HAD moved any more slowly, it would've stopped.

Chances were, Harper was going to bail.

But he had to take that chance.

A part of him sensed that she wanted to say yes but something held her back.

Did she truly want to shack up with a man old enough to be her grandfather?

Six o'clock finally came and he exited his door to knock on Harper's.

His heart felt stuck in his throat as he waited for the door to open.

When nothing happened, he swallowed and knocked a little more loudly.

Silence.

He leaned in and listened more intently for movement of any kind.

It was quiet as a tomb in there from what he could tell.

Son of a bitch. He'd been stood up. Teagan shook his head at Harper's balls.

Another door opened and Vanessa appeared, looking well put together as usual, her red lipstick an invite for sin. "Oh, honey, you look like someone just kicked your dog. What's wrong?"

"I got stood up, I think."

"You? Stood up? Who is this silly girl and is she blind?"

Teagan chuckled at Vanessa's defense of him and said, "You look good enough to eat. Got a date?"

"Actually, I do," she said, blushing just a little. "Do you remember the old fella I invited to go on the slide with me?"

"Yeah, Stuart something or other."

"Yes, Stuart Buck. Very nice man. I like him, even if he's a little old-fashioned. It's kinda cute, actually. Anyway, he invited me to dinner in the Mermaid Lounge. You should come, too. There's going to be dancing tonight."

"I'm not exactly dressed for dancing," he said ruefully, gesturing to his casual shorts and T-shirt. "And I don't want to horn in on your date. I doubt you need a third wheel."

"Nonsense. Go change. I'll wait."

He'd brought a suit, though he'd never thought he'd actually have cause to wear it. Maybe this would give him a chance to get to know Stuart better, to beat Harper at her own game. What the hell, he was here to make friends, right? "Give me two minutes," he said and disappeared into his room.

True to his word, he returned to Vanessa and received an approving smile. "Oh, honey pie, that girl is missing out."

She linked her arm through Teagan's and they walked to the Mermaid Lounge where Stuart was waiting.

The Mermaid Lounge was awash in hues of blue and green, evoking the sensation they were underwater. A large ice sculpture of a dolphin dominated the table of hors d'oeuvres and people mingled about before dinner was served.

Vanessa spied Stuart and waved, her eyes lighting up. Teagan was happy to note that the feeling seemed mutual as the older man made his way toward them.

"You look like a heart attack waiting to happen," Stuart said, admiring Vanessa's sequined dress. "I'm going to be the most envied man here."

Vanessa chuckled. "Oh, you sweet-talker." But it was clear Vanessa enjoyed the flattery.

The irony was hilarious. Harper wanted Stuart; Stuart wanted Vanessa; Vanessa had started off wanting Teagan and Teagan wanted Harper.

What tangled webs.

Speaking of.

As if a magnet was buried in his forehead, he zeroed in on Harper. She was wearing a black dress that clung to her curves, but unlike the white dress in the boutique, this one was classy.

And she was killing it.

Harper was scanning the crowd, no doubt looking for Stuart. He slipped through the crowd to come up behind her, sliding his arm around her waist, startling her. "You stood me up," he murmured against the shell of her ear.

She sucked in a quick breath and said, "I never agreed to a date. You shouldn't make assumptions."

He chuckled, taking careful note how a subtle shiver rocked her body. "Caught a chill?" Teagan teased, knowing full well it wasn't a chill that caused her to shake. "Lucky for you, all's well that ends well. I have an open spot at my table for you."

Teagan released her and moved in front, daring her to turn him down.

She met his gaze with a subtle smile playing on her lips. "Maybe I'm already meeting someone."

"You are. Me."

"Not you," she countered with a small laugh. "Someone else."

"Impossible."

"Your ego is quite healthy isn't it?"

"So is my libido."

Color flushed her cheeks a pretty pink. "What makes you think I'm interested in you like that?"

Teagan reached over to lightly caress the goose bumps still rioting on her arm. "Because your body tells me so."

Harper rubbed at her skin. "It's cold in here."

"Try again."

But Harper was as stubborn as she was beautiful. "Don't you have someone else you can stalk?"

"When you are so entertaining? Never. Now take my arm like a good girl and I'll take you to our table."

Harper looked conflicted—she really wanted to go with him but she also probably wanted to tell him to pound sand—and he enjoyed every minute of her consternation.

The little vixen deserved to have her feathers ruffled.

Harper took one final scan around the room, her mouth tightening with mild frustration, and turned to Teagan. "Fine, but only because the person I was hoping to see doesn't seem to be here yet."

"Oh, did you get stood up, too?"

Harper scowled. "I don't get stood up."

He laughed. "Now whose ego is healthy?"

She risked a small laugh. "My record speaks for itself."

"I'm sure it does," he agreed and walked her to the table where Stuart and Vanessa were already seated. To Harper, he said, "Harper, may I introduce Vanessa Vermuelen and Stuart Buck."

Harper's quick look of shock was skillfully smothered as she smiled. "Mr. Buck and I have already met. Pleasure to see you again."

Vanessa graced Stuart with a questioning expression and Stuart was quick to explain. "I accompanied the young lady on a stroll around the ship. She was lovely company."

Teagan wanted to crow. Stuart didn't seem all that taken with Harper in the way she'd hoped. But he didn't think for a moment that she would take defeat so easily.

"Yes, as were you," Harper returned smoothly. "We'll have to try it again sometime."

"That's sweet, honey, but you shouldn't spend all your time with my old bones when you've got this young stud right here," Stuart said, winking at Teagan.

Ha! Stuart was a good wingman.

Harper smiled, though Teagan could almost sense the disappointment seeping through her pores.

Good. The girl needed a little rejection to correct her attitude. At this rate, she was going to nose-dive into a canyon.

As he'd guessed, Harper was anything but defeated. "Stuart, please, I find wisdom and experience far more intriguing than the short-lived attributes of youth."

"That's a smart girl, right there," Vanessa chimed in, and Teagan nearly laughed at the irony again. If only Vanessa knew how Harper was trying to move in on Vanessa's new man. "Well, sit down, honey. Let's get to know each other."

But as Harper went to sit in the chair beside Stuart, Teagan expertly maneuvered her into the chair beside him, putting himself right in the way.

He smiled benignly at Harper but she knew full well he'd done it on purpose.

And there was no way in hell she'd call him on it without exposing her blatant interest.

Instead, Harper graced Teagan with a tight smile and sat gracefully in the offered chair.

"Aren't you two the cutest?" Vanessa exclaimed, tickled

at playing matchmaker. "Now, I will say, you are two of the most adorable people I've seen in ages. You should get married and make babies, right now."

Teagan blinked—*whoa there, Vanessa, slow your roll*—and coughed as he chuckled. "Not quite ready for that. I barely know this girl. For all I know, she's a terrible person with a pretty face."

Harper flushed and actually dropped her fake smile for a warning look that he found sexier than hell—though she probably hadn't meant to charge his batteries in that way—and returned with a sweetness he could choke on, "Darling, the same could go for you. Flyboys are notorious players. I'd hate to have my heart broken."

Have to have a heart to break it, he wanted to quip but he didn't.

Vanessa came to his defense again. "Sweetheart, Teagan is the real deal. I haven't known him long but I have a sixth sense about people. Teagan is a catch."

"I'm sure for the right person, he's a real…prize," Harper said, and Teagan could almost hear the sarcasm beneath the seemingly benign comment. "But for me, I prefer my partners to be more…*sophisticated*."

"Funny you should say that, because I prefer my ladies to be more down-to-earth. Less fussy."

Stuart nodded in agreement. "My beloved wife, Rachel, God rest her soul, was the salt of the earth. Didn't paint her face with all that gunk women use now and preferred to bake a pie rather than spend hours at the galleria. Hard to find another woman like her."

"Have you tried creating a clone?" Vanessa chimed in with a roll of her eyes. Stuart regarded her quizzically and Teagan wanted to warn Vanessa that she was about to lose her man if she kept talking, but Vanessa was a stubborn woman and she kept on going. "Look, honey, I'm happy as a clam that you had a good marriage and it worked for you, but seeking the same person as your wife isn't fair to the next woman. You ought to try looking for someone who is the opposite. Might find that you like something different."

"At my age, I know what I like," Stuart said gently, but Vanessa was already talking.

"And you know what? For years I thought I liked asparagus because my husband, Dale, loved the stuff. So I made it for him and I ate it right alongside him. But you know what? I hate asparagus. Tastes funny and makes your pee smell. So, I don't eat it anymore and I've been happier ever since."

Teagan quickly agreed, if only to have Vanessa's back. "Good point," he said, but then he added deliberately for Harper's benefit. "Life's about trying new things. Sometimes we can get in a rut, always chasing what we thought we wanted because it's what we always got. Change is good."

Vanessa clapped with enthusiasm, her smile infectious. "Exactly! You get it."

"Aren't you the philosopher," Harper murmured for Teagan's ears only, and he could practically hear her teeth grinding.

He grinned, fully enjoying tweaking Harper's nose.

Messing with Harper's game was the best entertainment he'd had in years.

10

WHAT WAS TEAGAN up to? Was he purposefully baiting her?

If she didn't know better, Harper would've sworn Teagan was onto her plan with Stuart and if so, he was actively trying to sabotage her.

The chilling thought danced on her taut nerves.

No, impossible. Maybe Teagan was just obnoxious and she was reading into his behavior out of her own panic.

But even if she were imagining things with Teagan, she was not imagining the connection that was quickly building between Stuart and his curvy guest.

The older woman was saucy, dark-haired and full of life. She looked like the kind of person who grabbed on to experiences and rode them into the dust.

Harper envied that sense of self.

In another world, another life, Vanessa was the kind of woman Harper could see herself looking up to.

But in this life, and this time, she was in the way.

Harper cleared her throat to add, "I think old-fashioned values are making a comeback. There's nothing better than a man with manners."

"A well-mannered man, yes, is a gem. But, honey, I've been around the block a few more times than you and I can say with great authority, sometimes when a man says he wants old-fashioned values, he wants a woman who's going to wait on him hand and foot. Trust me, I know because I was married to one for thirty years. Personally, I like a man who doesn't need a woman to do everything for him because he's perfectly capable of getting his own cup of coffee."

Harper caught Teagan's smile and she wanted to glare at him for being so smug. "Of course," Harper said, clarifying. "I'm just saying some of us still enjoy the idea of being a homemaker."

At that Teagan actually bust out laughing. "You're not saying that *you* want to be a homemaker, right? Because honey, no one at this table is buying that."

"And why not?" she demanded, trying not to stab him with her fork. "Perhaps you shouldn't judge by appearances."

But damn him, somehow he seemed to know when she was lying. She wasn't a homemaker any more than she was Betty Crocker. But if Stuart wanted a homemaker, she would be a homemaker. At least until the ring was on her finger and the ink was dry on the wedding certificate.

Teagan chuckled. "I'd wager a guess those hands of yours haven't washed a dish in at least five years."

"Because I take care of my hands, I'm not capable of washing a dish?"

Vanessa laughed, enjoying the growing tension between Harper and Teagan, misreading it for something else. "Oh, you two are like an old married couple who still have that spark. That there is called sexual tension." She turned to Stuart with merriment in her eyes. "Wouldn't you say these two kids have some crazy chemistry?"

Stuart laughed, seeing the humor in the situation. "There is definitely some energy between those two. Very entertaining."

Harper wanted to groan. This was not working at all. She didn't want Stuart looking at her like some young kid squabbling with her high school boyfriend. She had to do some damage control, fast.

"Stuart, how does a man like yourself—a gentleman—find yourself single? How was it that you haven't been snatched up by some smart lady by now?"

But dammit, Vanessa latched right on to Harper's question with one of her own.

"That's a pretty darn good question. Tell us, Stuart, any skeletons in your closet we should know about?"

Playing along, Stuart said, "Only the skeletons of my former business partners."

Vanessa laughed, enjoying his humor. "That's something my Dale would say. But I know you're nothing like Dale was in business. Dale would've cut the throat of his mother for a good deal."

"I daresay I wouldn't assault my mother—God rest her soul—but I do enjoy a good deal."

Good God, the banter was supposed to be between Harper and Stuart not Stuart and Vanessa. Her frustration growing, Harper pretended to perk up as the band played a catchy tune. "I love this band. Would you like to dance?"

But before Stuart could accept or decline, Vanessa jumped in again, pretending to scold Teagan.

"What is wrong with you, boy? This young lady wants to dance, get out there and show her a good time."

Stuart nodded, agreeing. "You two go out there and tear the dance floor up. I think I'll take this pretty lady for a spin."

Teagan's Cheshire grin made her want to howl but she had to save face. "Shall we?" she asked, and Teagan solicitously accepted her offer with fake humility.

"You don't have to ask me twice."

He grasped her hand and shock waves traveled up her arm, further stymieing her attempt to appear unaffected by anything Teagan said or did, at least in Stuart's presence.

If only that were true.

Teagan was quickly getting under her skin.

Once they were out of earshot, Harper snarled, "What do you think you are doing?"

Teagan's arm circled around her lower back, pressing her close. "Is that a trick question, because I thought we were dancing. Are you feeling all right, you look a little flushed."

"I'm fine. But you know I wanted to dance with Stuart. Why can't you get it through your head that I am not interested in you?"

"See, now here's the thing, I think you're lying through your pretty teeth. You are interested in me but you're too stubborn to admit it."

Her heart rate fluttered even as she wanted to stomp on his instep. "You are so full of it that I don't know if you suffer from some type of personality disorder or you're just dumb as a brick."

Her insult bounced off without injury. "Funny you should say that, because I've also wondered whether or not you suffer from some kind of disorder."

Harper's jaw dropped. "What is that supposed to mean?"

"Well, I have to ask myself, why would a woman like you actively chase after a man old enough to be her grandfather. My first option is that you're a gold digger and trying to get your sharp claws into the older man. My second option is that you have some weird fetish born out of a misplaced yearning for your daddy's affection. So either way, you chasing after Stuart isn't pretty. Honestly, I'm not sure which option is worse."

Harper swallowed the hot words that danced on her tongue because she knew engaging would only give him an advantage. "I don't know what you're talking about," she said stiffly. "Isn't it possible that I just enjoy his company more than I enjoy yours?"

Teagan didn't even hesitate to shoot her down. "You and I both know that's crap. How about this, let's try honesty. Lies are hard to keep straight."

"I have no idea what you're talking about. You don't know me well enough to say that I'm lying about anything."

Teagan pulled her closer. The sharp mint of his breath tickled her cheek and the warmth of his solid body threatened to melt hers like wax under a steady flame. Teagan was the kind of man who would ruin everything she had put into place thus far if she wasn't careful.

"Didn't your mama ever teach you that there's more to a woman's value than what's between her legs?"

Harper stiffened, hating that his comment had hit a chord. The thing was, her mother hadn't taught her that. If anything, Anna had taught the opposite, but that wasn't Teagan's place to intrude. "I don't see how that's any of your business."

"You're right, it's not my business, but if you continue to chase after that poor old man, I'll make it my business."

And there it was. The gauntlet thrown in challenge.

"Why do you care? You didn't even know the man until you met him on this boat," she pointed out.

"True. But you know what? I'm tired of people like you running over others to take what they didn't work for."

"Are you trying to suggest that the men I date are some helpless victims? You're an idiot if you think that."

"I don't know anything about the men in your past. All I know is that, that man over there is a nice guy. And I want you to leave him alone."

"Well too bad. I think he's a grown man and he can make his own decisions. I don't think he needs you to run point for him."

Teagan shrugged. "You could be right. Doesn't change what I'm going to do."

So, in a nutshell, Teagan had just admitted to openly trying to sabotage any effort she had toward Stuart. Why? "Are you trying to put him with Vanessa?"

"That match would make more sense," he replied.

"Do tell."

To that, Teagan met her gaze, his penetrating stare poking at her conscience. "Because unlike you, I know Vanessa really likes Stuart for who he is, not for what he can give her."

Harper tried not to feel small. She'd long ago shed any skin that resembled guilt. But it was hard to ignore the message that Teagan had just slapped across her forehead.

And it wasn't comfortable.

She blinked, afraid that tears weren't far behind. The knowledge both terrified and annoyed her. She was not a crier, by nature.

But before she could say anything in her own defense, Teagan swept a kiss across her lips, igniting a firestorm of epic proportions.

A kiss from the wrong guy.

She should've pushed Teagan away.

She should've at least made some sound of disgust as his firm lips traveled across hers.

But she was suspiciously silent.

Unless that tiny, mewling gasp counted for anything.

Yeah…it counted.

Damn him.

It counted a lot.

Teagan hadn't planned to kiss Harper, but that was the best part about spontaneous actions—they took both of you by surprise.

Maybe he'd kissed her because he'd wanted to see what she would do.

Or maybe he'd just wanted to taste that sass.

Either way, once he'd started, he wasn't ready to quit.

The dance floor disappeared, leaving only Harper and Teagan.

Their bodies meshed together perfectly, her softness complemented his strength. It took everything in him to not throw her over his shoulder and carry her to his room like a caveman.

But somehow, Teagan remembered they weren't alone.

That they were actually surrounded by people and that Stuart and Vanessa were, no doubt, watching and giggling at how they'd successfully matched them up.

If only they knew how Harper wanted nothing more than to toss him overboard.

At least when his mouth wasn't on hers.

Teagan regretfully broke the kiss and found Harper dazed, her lips glistening from his kiss.

"That's a good look on you," he murmured, breaking the spell.

Her gaze cleared and she hit him with a scowl worthy of a nun about to administer justice in Catholic school.

"Don't you ever do that again," she said, her tone just a tad too breathy to be convincing. "If we weren't surrounded by people, I'd kick you in the nuts."

"So bloodthirsty," he said, chuckling. "Are you into the rough stuff? I gotta admit, it's not my thing but I'd be willing to try it out at least once for you."

She gasped as his intentional misunderstanding, her cheeks coloring prettily. "You know that's not what I meant, you toad. I meant don't kiss me again."

"Just so I'm clear, you did not enjoy my lips on yours?"

"No." Her emphatic answer was supposed to be convincing, but the subtle shake in her arms told a different story. "No," she repeated, lifting her chin as if that made her point.

"So, you don't want me to do this, either," he whispered, slowly sliding his hand down to her pert behind, resting on the succulent cheek and giving it a firm squeeze as if he owned the woman attached to it.

"Um, no," she squeaked, rising up on her tiptoes, forcing her to cling to him more tightly.

"And then, that's a definite no, that you don't want me to do this…" His lips traveled the soft column of her skin where her bare shoulder met her neck, nipping and tasting as he went. "Mmm, you taste like summer strawberries," he murmured, the delightful discovery an unexpected admission.

"A-and you smell like—"

"Fate?"

"A—"

"A sinful good time?"

Teagan surreptitiously ground his bold erection against her belly, causing her to gasp. "A savage beast!" she finished, as if that were an insult.

"I'll take that," Teagan accepted with pride. "There are worse things. Such as my brother J.T.'s sweaty gym socks. Those reek. I mean, kill-a-small-country reek. So, yeah, I'll take savage beast any day."

"You're impossible," she groaned as he gracefully twirled her out and back into his arms. She moved like fingers under silk, smooth and without a snag. Together, their rhythm was almost flawless. "I want to sit down now."

"Not yet. We have an audience," he whispered in her ear. She glanced around and realized, yes, indeed, people were watching them command the dance floor. And because Harper, as he was quick to note, was highly competitive, she wasn't about to stop if people were feeding her need to win.

Teagan grinned, practically reading her mind. "Is everything a competition in your mind?"

"Isn't it in yours?" she returned coolly before dazzling with a smile that was meant for the crowd, but Teagan wasn't going to quibble. She was a showstopper and she was in his arms.

Thank God for the salsa lessons he'd taken many years ago. At least he knew some moves to keep her on her toes.

But she was a fast learner and kept pace.

They danced, spinning, working up a sweat as the motions were both sensual and vigorous. Harper made Teagan feel invisible as he twirled her around, lifted her off her feet and held her close.

They made a good pair.

Perhaps too good.

What had started out as his mission to mess with Harper had quickly turned into a raging sensual fever.

And he wasn't the only one suffering.

Harper's eyes flashed with unadulterated exhilaration as she landed in his arms and he dipped her with flourish.

Applause erupted throughout the lounge and Harper rose to smile shyly, waving to the crowd. Teagan upped the ante by kissing the back of her hand, like the gentleman she professed to want.

Their gazes locked and Teagan knew the attraction—as much as she tried to protest—was mutual. The heat radiating from her body pinked her cheeks and flushed her lips.

"Never let it be said that I don't pay attention," he said, letting the devil come out and play in his expression. The way her breath hitched and her pupils dilated, Teagan knew he'd pushed all the right buttons.

Whether she liked it or not.

11

HARPER EXCUSED HERSELF to go to the ladies' room to catch her breath.

What was happening?

She wet a paper towel and used it to blot her face, cooling down. Teagan was an amazing dancer.

Of course he was.

The man was probably an accomplished chef, too.

He flew planes.

Fought for our country.

Had a smile that was practically kryptonite.

And those lips…

She closed her eyes for a moment and savored the memory of Teagan's kiss.

How could something so small make her want to tear her clothes off?

It wasn't as if she'd never been kissed by a man who knew how to do it.

Harper scoffed at the thought, blotting her hairline and patting her neck where his lips had traveled and nipped.

But the shiver at the memory was telling.

You're a button-pusher, Teagan. She shook her head. *But you're not about to keep pushing mine.*

All was not lost.

Not yet, anyway.

She just needed some alone time with Stuart.

Which was hard to manage with Vanessa around the man all the time.

Maybe if she could find a substitute for Vanessa to spend some time with, it would free Stuart up to spend some quality time with Harper.

Not going to be easy with Teagan actively working against her, though.

She bit her lip.

Unless she also found someone for Teagan to spend time with.

Ugh. What was she turning into? The ship's love doctor?

Finally somewhat calm, Harper rinsed her hands a final time and began to exit the bathroom, only to run into Vanessa.

"Honey, I thought I'd check on you. That was some hot stuff out there. You'll have to teach me some of those moves."

"Honestly, it was Teagan," she admitted with a brief smile. Harper didn't want to like Vanessa but the woman had a way about her that drew people. And maybe it'd been too long since Harper had enjoyed a female friendship, much less a mother figure. Not that she was looking for either.

"Well, either way, you looked good out there. What I wouldn't give for those long legs of yours," Vanessa chuckled.

"You're very beautiful," Harper said. "But you know that."

Vanessa laughed as she reapplied her lipstick, then after carefully blotting and tossing the tissue in the trash, she turned to Harper. "Honey, have you ever been looking for something and swear you're never gonna find it, but then you realize, too late, that it's standing right in front of you?"

This smacked of a life lesson. Harper waited politely for Vanessa to make her point.

"Teagan is a good man. You could do worse."

"Unfortunately, he's not my type."

"Bullshit, honey. He's exactly the type you need."

"Come again?"

"Let's level with each other," Vanessa said. "I know you think you've got eyes for Stuart and I'm not going to stand in your way if that's the way the wind is blowing, but you're barking up the wrong tree. You need a man who will stand up to you, make you see stars and red at the same time. Stuart isn't that man."

Harper forced a smile because she didn't want to be rude, but she hated that everyone on this damn boat seemed to know what she was about, except the one man who only saw her as a kid. "My last lover was sixty-nine. I just like older men. Teagan doesn't have the seasoning I prefer. I hope that doesn't cause hard feelings between you and me."

"I just hate to see a young lady as pretty as you waste your time on something that's bound to bring you heart-ache."

"Stuart would never break my heart," Harper returned with confidence. She was the heartbreaker, not the other way around.

"Girls like you don't know what they want until it's too late to grab it," Vanessa said with a sad shake. "But Stuart isn't mine. We're just enjoying each other's company. He's free to spend time with whomever he chooses."

"Thank you. I'm pleased to hear you say that," Harper said, though she felt weird discussing this topic so openly. "May the best woman win?"

Vanessa's laugh was airy and bright as she exited the bathroom. "Honey, there was never any competition to win." Which left Harper to wonder if Vanessa was saying Harper didn't stand a chance or if Vanessa wasn't interested in play-ing.

Suddenly, Harper's head hurt.

Women were so complicated.

It would be so much easier if Vanessa had just screeched, "Stay away from my man, you little hussy!" because Harper knew how to handle that kind of confrontation.

Instead, Vanessa had messed with Harper's head by being kind, compassionate, a little sassy and wise, and possibly a little dangerous.

Under normal circumstances, Harper would've ruthlessly edged the woman out.

But…she liked Vanessa.

Even if she hadn't a clue what to think of her.

AFTER DINNER, VANESSA and Stuart went off on their own, mentioning they were going to check out the shuffleboard. While Harper's sharp disappointment in not being invited to join was hard not to enjoy, Teagan offered his arm for a walk around the starry deck.

To his surprise, she accepted.

Harper looped her arm through his with a decided pout that bordered on a scowl.

"You're lucky that you're pretty cute when you're acting like a baby," he said.

"I am not acting like a baby," she retorted, but Teagan sensed it was for show. For all her outward confidence, Harper's eyes gave away the lost soul she tried to hide. It was that part of her that intrigued him most. She sighed and leaned against him. "Why are you working against me? I don't understand. Why do you care?"

"I already told you," he answered, enjoying the warmth of her body against his arm. "People should hook up organically and there's no way you and Stuart would naturally meet up. I don't think it's right."

"Is it right for you to pass judgment on me? You don't know my story. Maybe I have a really good reason for doing what I do."

"There's never a good reason to use people."

She fell silent. Maybe she agreed. Maybe she wanted to tell him to shut up.

"I'm not a bad person."

"I never said you were."

"Why did you kiss me?"

"Because I wanted to." Teagan tried to remain nonchalant, but his heart rate was already quickening just by having Harper near. He wanted to taste all of her, not just her lips. Harper tilted his world and he wasn't quite sure how to right it.

"Do you always just take what you want?"

"Of course not."

She glanced up at him. "What if I would've screamed?"

"You didn't."

"But I could've."

"But you didn't."

Perhaps he'd taken a big risk in kissing her. But his gut had told him she was on the same page, even if she was fighting tooth and nail not to be. Sometimes sexual attraction, chemistry, all that stuff, didn't respond to rules.

They were alone on the deck. The damp breeze had a subtle chill to it, but the stars were brilliant against the dark velvet skies.

Hell, it was pretty damn romantic.

Harper drifted away from him to lean against the railing and he followed.

The wind played with her hair, causing his fingers to itch to touch it.

"What's your story?" she asked, curious. "Who are you, Teagan Carmichael?"

"Just a guy. Simple dreams, simple needs. Nothing more to me than that."

"Don't you ever want more?"

"I've had more. Didn't make me feel any better about the stuff I was trying to forget. A full bank account does nothing for a troubled mind."

"That's very Chinese fortune cookie of you," she retorted, turning away to face the open sea. "Some of us don't have the luxury of living like monks."

Teagan chuckled, coming to stand right behind her, sliding his hands around her waist. "Forgoing designer bags and weekly pedicures isn't living like a monk."

"Maybe not for you."

"Pretty toes are important to you?"

She turned in his arms to gaze up at him. "When it comes to women, pretty toes, pretty everything, are important to *men*."

"Not me."

Teagan thumbed her soft cheek, bending to brush his lips against hers. She opened her mouth and he deepened the kiss. There was something so sweet about the way her tongue darted, as if unsure, against his, tasting, testing. The tiny soft gasps and moans nearly killed him.

He could kiss her all night.

But that wouldn't change the fact that she was a gold digger and he wasn't in the right tax bracket.

Teagan regretfully broke the kiss first.

"You know this doesn't change anything, right?" she said.

"You mean, as in, you're still going to chase down Stuart Buck as your prize?" he answered with a wry grin.

"Something like that." Harper nodded but added, "However, if we both agree that nothing is going to change and we're both free to go after whomever we want, who's to say we couldn't enjoy each other's company right now?"

Was Harper propositioning him?

"Is this where I say, 'I'm not that kind of boy'?"

She glanced up at him coyly. "I don't know. Are you?"

Instead of answering, he countered, "And what if I said one night with me and you'll keep coming back for more?"

Harper laughed at his boast. "I'd say you shouldn't get your hopes up. I'm offering one night. No strings. Workout-the-tension kind of release for us both. Are you up for that?"

If his raging erection were any judge—he was exactly up for that.

And anything else she could throw at him.

Teagan grasped her hand with a grin and said, "Challenge accepted, pretty girl."

He was about to show her that money couldn't buy stamina.

Or the equipment he was working with.

Thank God J.T. had stuffed a box of condoms in his bag before leaving.

They were going to make a serious dent in that box tonight.

12

HARPER KNEW GOING with Teagan was a mistake, but it felt so good to do something she wanted to do for once.

She knew there was no future with the man leading her to his room and she was okay with that.

All she wanted was to lose herself in the arms of someone of her own choosing.

Teagan's room was more like a suite, though still cozy, as most staterooms were on a cruise ship.

Suddenly nervous, Harper opened her mouth to suggest a drink first but Teagan shared no such trepidation.

"Oh!" she exclaimed as Teagan hoisted her into his arms. Her legs immediately wrapped around his trim waist and locked in place as he hungrily launched at her mouth with a kiss that stole her breath.

Harper gasped against his mouth, everything inside her churning with heat and need. Teagan was a master with his tongue, driving inside her mouth, tasting, teasing, and it was near impossible not to shudder with anticipation at what else he could do.

Gone was the charming stranger with the wry smiles and twinkling eyes.

This guy—the guy pressing her against the wall, grinding that thick length against her groin—was ready to make good on his promise that she would leave wanting more.

She'd never felt so needed, so desired.

His hands, firm and strong, moved with the assurance of a man who knew what he wanted and didn't hesitate to go after it.

Harper shivered, losing herself to the sensation of being consumed by a man who took no prisoners in their sensual war.

Teagan's mouth traveled the column of her neck, igniting the nerve endings with a nip of his teeth as he teased the soft flesh. Harper bit her lip to keep from begging for more.

Every inch of her body was alive and tingling with an incessant need for Teagan's touch.

She'd always been the seductress—always needed to dazzle her potential lovers with fantastic sex so they were blinded to anything but her—but she wasn't pretending this time.

Every moan, every gasp, every shudder was one hundred percent genuine. She couldn't even muster the brain power to embellish her pleasure. Teagan was the real deal.

How did she know?

Because all he'd done was kiss her like a savage and she was ready to lose herself.

Harper wrenched her mouth away. "Are we going to do this or not?" she asked in a husky, sex-starved tone that didn't even sound like her, but she was becoming desperate for the need to feel him inside her.

"Impatient little minx," he chuckled, walking her to the bed dominating the bedroom.

"Foreplay bores me," she lied.

"Then you've been doing it wrong," Teagan replied, tossing her to the bed with a dark grin. In those beautiful eyes she saw a promise of unending pleasure and it both scared her and turned her on. Teagan reached under her black dress and slowly inched her panties down her thighs. "I don't rest until my woman is wet, panting and clawing to get at my cock. That's when I know she's ready for me."

"And why is that?" she said, holding her breath as Teagan tossed her panties aside and shimmied her dress up over her hips so he could get to what he really wanted.

His lazy smile was both devilish and dark—a combination she'd never seen look so sexy. "Because slippery is better, baby, when you're packing heat."

Harper started to laugh—every guy thought he was bigger than the last—but as Teagan dropped his shorts and shucked his briefs, the laughter dried in her throat as she sat straight up and stared.

"That's not going to fit," she said with absolute certainty, but the tingle in her belly encouraged her to try. "Oh, my God, I'll never be the same again! You should have to register that thing as a concealed weapon."

Teagan laughed and pulled her legs toward him as he knelt at the edge of the bed between her thighs. "That's why slippery is better."

If Harper had half a mind to rethink the situation, Teagan didn't give her a chance.

That tongue…the one that'd ratcheted up the heat level with a searing kiss, was now right at her hot spot, folds parted and seeking that engorged button.

Harper clutched at the bedspread, unable to catch her breath.

"Oh, God, Teagan," she panted, unable to control the guttural moans spilling from her mouth. The intensity grew with steady pressure as Teagan pushed her to the edge, then drew her back, only to drive her harder. The telltale quake of her thighs told her she was seconds from coming. Teagan knew it, too, the devil. She should've known the observant bastard would key in on her cues effortlessly. It was as if he had a blueprint to her erogenous zones and he was merciless in his pursuit.

Harper clenched in almost painful pleasure as she climaxed, toes curling, voice strangled in the most intense sensual crash of her life.

Dazed, she was barely aware of anything until she saw Teagan looming above her, his lips glistening from her juices, his cock sheathed in latex, dragging against her belly. He lowered to kiss her deeply, her scent clinging to his mouth as he toyed with her tongue.

"Your pussy tastes like sugared vanilla," he said, against her mouth. "I'd eat you for dessert anytime."

A delighted flush heated her cheeks at the obscene compliment. There was something so hot about the dirty way he talked in private, which was so different from the man she'd first met.

Teagan moved onto his knees, and hooked her legs over his shoulders as he positioned that heat-seeking missile toward her entrance.

He was going to bend her in half and impale her on that thing.

And she couldn't wait.

If she could squirm with anticipation, she would, but he had her locked in place.

There was no escaping what was coming.

TEAGAN SLOWLY FED his length into her slick passage, taking the time to let her adjust as he pushed forward.

In her entire life she'd never been so filled by a man.

The sensation was heady and powerful.

And then, when she feared she couldn't take another inch, he was fully seated inside her, stretching and filling until she was aware of only Teagan.

His cock rubbed unerringly against her G-spot and she nearly cried as the pleasure erupted almost immediately.

Teagan thrust against her with measured movements, gauging her reaction, watching as she tried to keep from succumbing so quickly to the pleasure.

They locked gazes. Her behind was nestled against his

groin as he was buried inside her. The heat between them was enough to scald. Electricity crackled in the tight space. Nothing existed but them.

Sweat dewed their bodies as they moved together.

The carnal concert in the room became more primal as each worked closer to that inevitable end.

Teagan's expression tightened as he gritted his teeth, his thrusts going deeper.

"Harper," he groaned, his voice rough. "Come for me, baby."

She shuddered, yielding to the orgasm rattling down her nerve endings and roaring through her bones.

Harper vaguely heard Teagan shout as he came.

A smaller ricochet pulsed through her body as a second orgasm hovered on the edge.

She groaned as Teagan reached between them and pinched her aching clit with just enough pressure to send her into orbit.

She may have shouted his name.

She may have blacked out.

Honestly, she couldn't rightly recall.

All she knew was that her body had never been so thoroughly satisfied by a man until Teagan.

Oh, God, that was not a good sign.

Not good at all.

COMING DOWN FROM that high left Teagan with a thundering heartbeat and an immediate need to nap.

He felt drained, but in a good way.

Was this what bliss felt like?

Not to wax too poetically about it, but…yeah, he was feeling pretty good.

He turned to his side to regard Harper, her eyes still closed, her mouth slack as she fought to catch her breath.

Hair tousled in the sexiest bed head he'd ever seen, he

found her relaxed, completely natural state far more alluring than the sex kitten part she played for others.

Harper's eyes opened slowly, meeting his gaze. His grin told the story. She blushed and covered her face with her hands because there weren't words. *How is that for the biggest ego boost, ever?*

"Let me know when you're ready for round two," he said, to which she groaned.

"Keep that anaconda to yourself," she said, trying to roll away but he caught her by the waist and pulled her straight to him. She laughed, pretending to be horrified when his semiflaccid cock leaped to life on her thigh.

"Aww, look, he likes you," Teagan said.

Harper's deep-throated laugh tickled his senses.

Sobering slowly, he asked, "Are you okay? I didn't hurt you, right?"

Harper shook her head shyly. "You didn't hurt me."

"I'm glad," he said. Having a big cock wasn't all fun and games. Sometimes it was a real nuisance. "Is it too cheesy to admit that we fit together pretty well?"

"Yes."

"Okay, well, I already put it out there. I like the way my *tab* fits in your *slot*," he said with a half grin. "You feel… perfect."

"Stop," she groaned, trying to hide her smile.

"Why?"

"You know why."

"Enlighten me."

Harper sighed and admonished him with a look. "You know this was a one-time thing. It's not like I'm going to start sneaking into your room for booty calls. So don't try to butter me up with flattery."

"Hey, don't get ahead of yourself. I didn't say I wanted booty calls. I'm just saying, it's rare for me to find a woman who can accommodate me like you can."

She wrinkled her nose in adorable embarrassment. "We can stop talking about it now."

"For a woman who uses sex to lure men, you're a little prudish."

"Prudish?" she repeated. "Hardly."

He laughed at her affront. "Honey, you can't even talk about what we've done together without blushing. Sex should be fun, exciting and adventurous."

"I have plenty of fun," she retorted, but Teagan found her bashfulness incredibly telling and alluring. *Hell, who am I kidding?* He found everything about Harper alluring.

"What's the wildest thing you've ever done in bed?" he challenged, loving the way she looked on her back next to him. Her perfect, plump breasts begged for his hands and those dusky nipples needed to be in his mouth, but he wanted to hear her stories. "C'mon, where's the harm?"

"I don't kiss and tell."

"I'm not asking for names. Just acts. What did you do?" He slid his palm down her belly, noting the minute tremors at his touch, and cupped her mound firmly. "I want to know how this sweet pussy right here has been properly taken. I'm all ears, baby."

Harper inhaled sharply as he slowly pushed his index finger between her damp folds to stroke her clit with feather-light touches.

She gasped as he left her clit to push his finger deeper to find her G-spot. "W-what are you doing? I can't think…"

Her nipples pearled and he dipped down to suck one into his mouth.

She threaded her fingers through his hair and clutched hard as he found a good spot to torture. Harper was so damn responsive. All it took was a few good strokes and she was shaking already, crying out, "Not again, oh God, ohh God…." And then she came again so sweetly, shuddering and mewling in short gasps as he gently withdrew his finger. She watched with a muzzy gaze as he sucked her flavor from his finger, smiling with pleasure at her unique taste.

"Now tell me," he instructed softly. "I want to know how wild you really are."

"I can't believe you want to know that," she said with a throaty laugh. "Why would you want to know what I've done with other men?"

"Because I have a feeling you haven't done anything worth remembering," he challenged as he nuzzled her neck. She gasped and hooked her arms around him. He moved over her, smiling down. "But that's easily remedied."

"Is that so?"

"Yes. I have many things I'd like to do to you. In every possible way, every possible position, every possible place."

Harper shivered beneath him but her smile widened. "And how is that going to happen when I've only agreed to this one time?"

"You and I both know, this is happening again," he said, brushing a brief kiss across her lips. "But if you want to pretend that you're still going to walk out that door and be done with this, then go ahead. I like to play games, too."

She lightly pinched his nipple. "That ego is going to bite you in the ass."

"It's not ego if it's fact."

Harper rolled her eyes. "You're impossible."

"I like to call it confident."

"You can call it what you like but that's all you're getting."

Her gaze went straight to his cock as he rose up on his knees. Teagan laughed and said, "Maybe if you weren't looking at my cock like that, I might believe you. But seeing as you look ready to eat me alive…yeah, I'm not buying that story."

Harper tried to roll away but he caught her legs and trapped her on her belly. That delectable ass begged for a kiss and he was ready to oblige. Pulling her toward him, she squealed with laughter as she tried to get away but he was much too strong.

"What are you doing?" she said, her laughter muffled by the bedspread. "Oh, my God, don't you dare!"

But it was already too late. There were some things in life you just couldn't resist—Harper's ass being one of them.

Teagan lifted her hips and brought that sweet behind to his mouth for a nibble.

"Oh, yes, that is one fine ass," he said, nipping at the tender flesh, eliciting squeals and gasps as he traveled across the rounded landscape, pausing even to delve his tongue between the valley of the twin halves. "The things I'm going to do to you…"

And that was a promise he couldn't wait to make good on.

13

HARPER GASPED, COLLAPSING on the bed after an epic round three.

Was it possible to die from too many orgasms?

The question wasn't entirely made in jest.

"No more," Harper begged, rolling to her side into a ball. Everything was pulsing and tingling, her body was alive in ways she'd never known, but she was exhausted.

She needed to leave Teagan's bed and get to her own, but the only way that was happening was if she crawled.

Teagan pulled her to his side, spooning her with a satisfied sigh.

"I shouldn't stay," she mumbled, but her eyelids were dropping already.

"Mmm-hmm," he replied, and she could almost see his eyes close.

"Don't get too attached," she warned.

"Right. Don't get attached," he recited, but she knew he was just saying whatever she wanted to hear. Unfortunately, she was too tired to make her point by getting up and leaving him in his bed to sleep alone.

If she didn't know better, she'd say he'd planned it that way.

They both fell instantly asleep but Harper awoke sometime before dawn and found the strength to sneak out.

Once safely in her own room, she closed her eyes and mentally counted to ten. Best sex of her life.

Hands-down.

But life was about more than good sex.

That's what vibrators were for.

Bone-melting orgasms didn't put money in her back account.

But money would never fill that yawning hole inside her heart that seemed to grow each year.

Not everyone got the fairy tale, that was the bottom line, and she wasn't going to spend her youth chasing after something she might never get.

Tiny muscle twinges reminded her abruptly of Teagan and her mouth ignored her brain and smiled at the memory.

Teagan…his touch, his scent, the way he mastered her body without being overbearing…she didn't know men like him actually existed outside of movies and books.

True, Harper had become jaded as of late. She rarely watched rom-coms or read love stories because she found herself rolling her eyes more often than not.

Men in real life didn't sweep the girl off their feet and ride off into the sunset together.

It made for great entertainment—for some—but it was unrealistic.

Love was for suckers.

A forlorn sigh escaped her lips. Someday Teagan would make some lucky woman pretty happy.

Not her, though.

So that's settled. You had your fun, now back to work.

Unlike everyone else, this wasn't a pleasure cruise for her.

If gold digging was a real profession, she'd count this cruise as a business expense on her taxes.

Today, they would cruise into port at Puerto Vallarta so everyone who was interested could shop and enjoy the sights for the day.

Harper fully intended to use this opportunity to get close to Stuart.

She knew that Stuart enjoyed cultural cuisine, so she'd already scoped out a top-notch restaurant to suggest to Stuart in the hopes of gaining some alone time.

But first, she needed to shower.

While she fully intended to remain focused, it was difficult to keep her thoughts on track when every slide of the soap reminded her of where Teagan's hands had been.

Harper kept in shape but her body had been given a thorough workout.

She was sore in places she hadn't realized had muscle.

Making quick work of the shower, she dressed, threw her hair up in a messy but stylish bun, and then perfected her face with light makeup—which included covering up the dark smudges under her eyes from a wild night, and a dab of lip gloss.

Satisfied with her reflection, she grabbed her purse and exited her room to go downstairs for poached eggs with Stuart.

But as she approached the breakfast area, Harper scowled when she realized someone had beat her to the table.

Stuart and his new bestie, Vanessa, were sitting a bit too close and laughing like teenagers.

"Seems a shame to break up that little party, doesn't it?"

The voice in her ear was unmistakable. She turned to face Teagan. "Are you stalking me? You're like an unlucky penny. You keep showing up when I least expect it."

"Is it unlucky? I seem to feel someone got very lucky last night. At least four times. Maybe it was five… I lost count."

Her cheeks flared with heat. "I'm not talking about that," she said under her breath. "I need you to stop following me around. I don't want Stuart to get the wrong idea."

"And that's exactly what I want Stuart to do," he countered, looping her arm through his and pulling her to the table with him.

"What are you doing?" she managed to hiss before they reached the group, but she pasted a bright smile for appearances as Teagan asked if they could join.

"Of course, sugar pie," Vanessa exclaimed, waving them over. "We're just gobbling our breakfast before our big adventure. I told Stuart he needs more than those stinky old eggs but he's a creature of habit, apparently."

"Eggs are a perfect protein," Stuart said, unfazed.

"Yes, but French toast is dessert for breakfast," Vanessa said, relishing her next bite with flourish. "Mmm. Life is for the living, doll face."

Harper accepted the seat Teagan had pulled out for her, but she wanted to kick him under the table.

She'd never had anyone actively sabotage her.

Especially someone she'd just had incredible sex with hours earlier. Vanessa's statement snagged Harper's attention. "Adventure?" she prompted with a puzzled smile.

Stuart grinned and gestured to Vanessa. "This wildcat has somehow talked me into zip lining with her when we dock for port."

"At your age?" Harper couldn't help but ask. "Are you sure that's safe?"

Vanessa laughed and waved away Harper's question. "Honey, if you're not living, you're dying. And Stuart needs to get to living. I added zip lining to his bucket list and lo and behold, Puerta Vallarta has some of the best. I say that's fate."

Stuart seemed to find Vanessa's logic sound, or at the very least entertaining. "How can I argue with that?"

But Harper certainly could try to point out the lunacy of such an excursion. "Forgive me, but zip lining in Mexico? Doesn't seem very safe. I don't know if they have the same safety precautions as they would in the States."

Teagan added his two cents. "Naw, it should be fine. They do a monster business with the tourists. Can't make money if they're killing people. I'm sure it's fine. Besides,

I've brought plenty of charter clients here and I know of a few good zip line excursions I could recommend."

Of course he does. Now Harper really wanted to kick him. She cast him a sharp look. "Yes, but it seems like an *unnecessary* risk. I was actually thinking of having lunch at La Casa Senorita, which I've heard is so authentic, that once you eat there, you'll never be able to stomach what we pass off as Mexican cuisine back home."

"What's wrong with zip lining?" Teagan pressed with a curious grin. "Scared?"

"Of course not," she lied. She was terrified of heights. And dying in the Mexican rain forest. "I just have different ideas of what an adventure might entail."

"I think you need to broaden your horizons," Teagan said.

"Well, I don't remember asking you," Harper said with a false smile. "Now, as I was saying—"

But it was Stuart who agreed with Teagan. "Honey, your fella is right. You're young. You should be tasting life, not spending your time doing things the safe way. Challenge yourself. That's what I'm doing for the first time in my life and I have to tell you, it's invigorating."

Vanessa piped in, "Come with us, sweetheart. I'm sure we can accommodate two more." She looked to Teagan. "How about it? Up to zipping through the canopy?"

"I'm always up for an adventure," Teagan said amiably, leaving her to look like the ass if she declined.

"I…" She licked her lips and tried to smile through her trepidation. If she backed out, she'd lose out on time with Stuart. But if she went through with it, Harper might just vomit, which was not sexy at all. "I…guess?" she finally said, wanting to fall through the floor.

Vanessa clapped with delight. "Very good," she said, pleased. "Now get to eating something because you're going to need it today."

Teagan smiled and handed Harper a breakfast roll with

an innocuous smile. "Yes, you look a little pale. Did you not get enough sleep last night?"

Harper bit into the roll just to keep from snapping at Teagan for orchestrating this nightmare.

The truth was, her palms were already sweating and she wanted to bolt.

But Harper wasn't a quitter.

If Stuart was zipping...so was she.

TEAGAN WANTED TO LAUGH. Harper looked as if she'd just been asked to swallow nails.

He resisted being impressed by her determination to see something through because her goal was messed up to begin with, but what could he say? She had a plucky spirit that he found adorable.

Even if she was not exactly a nice person.

Breakfast passed quickly and Harper was suspiciously quiet, choking down those poached eggs as if it were her duty, and then when everyone was finished, she excused herself to freshen up.

He thought to follow her, but that was going a bit far.

Vanessa leaned over to Teagan. "Is everything okay with Miss Hot Stuff?"

Teagan laughed as he shrugged. "I'm not privy to that information."

"Oh, don't con me, pretty boy. You two have tension."

You have no idea, he wanted to quip, but he remained respectfully silent. He didn't like to kiss and tell, either. As if he needed a reminder that he hadn't gotten enough sleep, a large yawn cracked his jaw. "Sorry," he apologized, rubbing his face. "I think I need more coffee."

"A good run in the morning will perk you right up," Stuart suggested. "I used to start my day with a good five miles until my knee gave out. Now the doctor has said I should stick to walking or swimming. Not quite the same."

"The only running I do is from estate sale to estate sale. I do love a bargain," Vanessa said. "Just the other day I found a rare German Black Forest cuckoo clock in a bin marked 'free' just because the mechanism needed a little tune-up."

Stuart perked up with astonishment. "You're sure it was authentic?"

"I had a hunch, but when I took it to my antiques dealer, he nearly fainted. So, yes, I'm pretty sure it's authentic."

"What a find," Stuart exclaimed, seeming to share Vanessa's enthusiasm. "What did you do with it?"

"I kept it," she admitted. "I had planned to sell it for a good profit, but I've always had a thing for clocks so…it's hanging in my office, annoying my dog when the little bird pops out to announce the time."

"I would love to see that," Stuart said, clearly interested. "My father was an amateur clockmaker and I inherited the bug as a hobby. If you're interested in clocks, you should see my collection."

Vanessa did a little shimmy shake with her shoulders, excited. "I will take you up on that offer. But for now, we are going to fly, baby. Are you ready?"

Stuart tossed his napkin on the table emphatically, his grin matching Vanessa's. "You bet I am."

Stuart rose and Vanessa placed her hand in his as she said to Teagan, "We'll see you at the dock, honey."

Harper returned just in time to see Vanessa and Stuart heading off in the opposite direction, still chatting and laughing as they went.

No longer needing to put on a front, Harper let her disappointment show.

"They have a lot in common," Teagan said, coming to stand beside Harper. "I think it's cute."

"Shut up."

Harper's dark look amused him. He rubbed the frown lines in the middle of her forehead. "Careful…wrinkles."

She swiped at his hand and exhaled in irritation. "I don't

understand. Why does a man his age want to do something so dangerous?"

"It's not that dangerous. It's not as if he's signed on to wrestle alligators in the Amazon. This is a typical tourist attraction. He'll be fine." He cast her a sidewise glance. "I'm touched that you care so much for Stuart's welfare. How very kind of you."

"I do care," she returned, lifting her chin. "I'm not a monster."

"Didn't say you were."

"You implied it."

"Nope." Teagan grinned, cutting Harper off just as she started to gather steam. "Oh, we'd better get moving. We've docked. We want to get the best outfitters for our adventure."

He grasped her hand firmly and pulled her along with him. Harper dragged her feet but didn't wriggle out of his grasp. If anything, she clutched him more tightly.

Could it be possible, Harper was scared?

She seemed so fearless, but Teagan knew sometimes people hid their fear well.

"You're so tense," he said as they walked to the exit corridor. "Maybe you need a massage. Sore muscles can make people grouchy."

"I'm fine," she snapped, and then, as if to prove a point, she shook his hand free. "We're not a couple. I told you... one night."

He laughed. "Such a stickler for the fine print."

"That's the way the world works."

"Yes, true enough. Good thing I'm pretty talented at finding loopholes."

Harper shot him a quick look. "There are no loopholes."

"We'll see. For now, let's just have fun."

"Easy for you to say," she grumbled with uncharacteristic worry. "Are you sure this is safe?"

"Pretty sure."

YOUR PARTICIPATION IS REQUESTED!

Dear Reader,

Since you are a lover of our books – we would like to get to know you!

Inside you will find a short Reader's Survey. Sharing your answers with us will help our editorial staff understand who you are and what activities you enjoy.

To thank you for your participation, we would like to send you 2 books and 2 gifts – **ABSOLUTELY FREE!**

Enjoy your gifts with our appreciation,

Pam Powers

SEE INSIDE FOR READER'S SURVEY

For Your Reading Pleasure...

We'll send you 2 books and 2 gifts
ABSOLUTELY FREE
just for completing our Reader's Survey!

YOUR READER'S SURVEY
"THANK YOU" FREE GIFTS INCLUDE:
▶ 2 FREE books
▶ 2 lovely surprise gifts

PLEASE FILL IN THE CIRCLES COMPLETELY TO RESPOND

1) What type of fiction books do you enjoy reading? (Check all that apply)
- ○ Suspense/Thrillers
- ○ Action/Adventure
- ○ Modern-day Romances
- ○ Historical Romance
- ○ Humor
- ○ Paranormal Romance

2) What attracted you most to the last fiction book you purchased on impulse?
- ○ The Title
- ○ The Cover
- ○ The Author
- ○ The Story

3) What is usually the greatest influencer when you <u>plan</u> to buy a book?
- ○ Advertising
- ○ Referral
- ○ Book Review

4) How often do you access the internet?
- ○ Daily ○ Weekly ○ Monthly ○ Rarely or never

5) How many NEW paperback fiction novels have you purchased in the past 3 months?
- ○ 0 - 2
- ○ 3 - 6
- ○ 7 or more

YES! I have completed the Reader's Survey. Please send me
the 2 FREE books and 2 FREE gifts (gifts are worth about $10 retail)
for which I qualify. I understand that I am under no obligation to
purchase any books, as explained on the back of this card.

150/350 HDL GLNY

FIRST NAME	LAST NAME

ADDRESS

APT.#	CITY

STATE/PROV.	ZIP/POSTAL CODE

HB-217-SUR17

"Pretty sure?" She skidded to a stop. "That's not very reassuring."

"I can say it's definitely safer than trying to jettison from a jet at high speed, hoping and praying your chute opens and you don't plummet to the ground and become a big splotch of mottled colors. Yeah, after that zip lining seems like cake."

"You've done that?" Harper asked, disbelieving. "Are you serious?"

"Yeah, that's one of the reasons I was ready to call it quits on my military career. One too many times flirting with death. I figured, eventually, if I kept pushing my luck, fate was going to win."

"That's intense."

"Oh, yeah. *Intense* is a good word for it."

Harper fell silent for a moment as they walked, and then she grudgingly offered, "Thank you for your service."

"You're welcome," he answered, feeling an odd twang of something deeper than pride at her gratitude. It meant something that she cared, even if she didn't want to admit it. But Teagan wasn't about to go all mushy, not yet, so he said, "And thank you for having the world's most perfect ass."

Harper gasped around an embarrassed smile and he chuckled, enjoying the way her eyes flashed with genuine pleasure.

He gave her props for sticking to a flawed battle plan, but too bad for Harper, because she'd already lost this war.

Tonight, Harper was going to be right where she was last night...

In his bed.

14

VANESSA, STUART, TEAGAN and Little Miss Hot Stuff sat among a group of fellow tourists in a cramped, modified school bus as they jounced along a dirt road toward their destination.

It was smelly, humid and uncomfortable, but Vanessa was soaking in the experience.

Harper, on the other hand, looked like a cat about to be thrown into a pool of water.

The kid's plans were pretty transparent. Pretty girl, used to getting her way, using her looks and figure to get what she wanted in life.

Vanessa didn't judge the girl.

Actually, she felt a kinship with Harper.

Weird that she would say that, considering Harper was actively trying to get her hooks into Vanessa's new buddy, but there was something about Harper that made Vanessa want to look out for her.

Maybe it was old age creeping up on her. Menopause did strange things to women's emotions.

Teagan was whispering something in Harper's ear, something sultry enough to make her blush, and Vanessa smothered a knowing laugh. Those two were a good match.

But Harper was going to fight tooth and nail against it.

That girl was broken inside.

And for that, Vanessa almost wanted to warn Teagan to keep his distance, but she knew from experience people didn't listen when their brains were shut off.

People had tried to warn Vanessa about Dale but she hadn't listened to that, either.

She'd been in *luvvvvvv*.

No, what she hadn't known then was that love would come later. Lust had been fueling her decisions at that time.

Yeah, loving Dale hadn't been easy but Vanessa had never been one to take the easy road.

She leaned over to Stuart who was holding on to the hand strap hanging from the ceiling for additional stability. "How you doing?"

"Good," he answered, though Vanessa was pretty sure he was hating the bus ride. "It's all part of the experience."

"Yes, it is," she agreed. "This bus ride is hell on the tush but what's life without a few bumps and bruises, right?"

Stuart smiled but readjusted his grip.

Vanessa had to admit, she was getting a soft spot for the old guy.

He was spry enough to warrant a second glance and they seemed to have more in common than she would've thought.

All this time she'd been chasing after younger guys, playing up the cougar angle, but hanging out with Stuart was a refreshing change.

They hadn't kissed or anything like that.

But Vanessa wasn't averse to giving it a try.

However, he had to make the first move. In some things, she remained a bit old-fashioned.

The bus rolled to a stop, jostling them like apples in a crate, and they gratefully disembarked.

She drew a deep breath of the sweet jungle air and enjoyed the vista. "Look at all that green," Vanessa said, pointing toward the canopy below them. "Gorgeous."

Stuart stood beside her, agreeing. "Very nice. Pristine, even."

Vanessa grabbed her phone and snapped a selfie of them together. "Memories, baby."

"I'd say send that to me, but I'd never figure out how to retrieve it. My secretary always has to show me how to work my phone."

Vanessa chuckled and patted his cheek. "Darlin', I'll take care of the tech on this trip. You just keep those toes twinkling because I expect another spin around the dance floor before this trip is done."

"Sounds like a bargain I can stick to," Stuart said, grinning.

Oh, for an older guy, he had the most impish smile. She rather liked that about him.

Actually, she liked a lot about Stuart Buck.

But, unlike Harper, her feelings had nothing to do with his money.

THE BUS DROPPED them off at a vista that wound down into the jungle from a narrow trail that looked too small for human feet, much less the mules that were waiting for them.

Teagan took to his mule right away, becoming the Horse Whisperer or something, whereas Harper's mule kept giving her a sideways look that told her to climb aboard at her own peril.

But seeing as Vanessa and Stuart and the rest of their party were already saddled up and ready to rock and roll, Harper had no choice but to tentatively swing her leg over and try to mount the damn thing.

As she feared, the mule had other plans and shifted away with a warning whinny.

The tour guide hustled over and tried to calm the beast, speaking rapidly in Spanish, but the animal wasn't having it.

After three attempts to get Harper on the mule, the tour

guide admitted it was probably a bad idea to force the mule to carry her.

The tour guide grinned widely as if this wasn't a problem and said, "You ride with friend."

Friend? A glimmer of hope surged as she looked toward Stuart, but he wasn't even paying attention to the fact that she was practically being trampled by a grumpy beast.

She bit her lip and caught Teagan's eye. He knew she had to ask him. She was almost tempted to sit in the bus and wait for them to return.

But Harper knew it was beyond stupid to be a woman alone on a deserted dirt road in Mexico, so she gritted her teeth and asked Teagan if she could share his mule.

"No problem," he said, reaching down to help her mount behind him. "Hold on tight."

She slid her arms around his waist and fought against the immediate thrill. Why was he so freakin' beautiful? He had the body of an Adonis. She had the crystal clear memories to remind her.

They settled into single file as they meandered down the path, the birds squawking and calling, filling the air with a cacophony of sound. It was hard not to be awed by the lush landscape. It was like a paint store exploded and color landed everywhere.

"Not an animal lover I take it?" Teagan said, making conversation.

"I like animals."

"So, you just wanted to ride with me?"

"Don't flatter yourself. My mule was grumpy. It was a safety issue." She shivered as his chuckle rumbled against her chest. "To further the point, I love horses, even."

"So that's why you're holding on to me for dear life?"

"Just shut up and pay attention to the road, please," she said, squeezing her eyes shut so she didn't have to see how precarious their path was through the wilds of Mexico.

This was not her idea of a good time.

Sipping fine wine, eating strawberries aboard a yacht, watching Netflix in her yoga pants…those were all great ways to spend the day.

This?

Not even in her top one hundred.

Except Teagan smelled really good.

She wrinkled her nose at the yumminess assaulting her nostrils, making it damn near impossible to forget how it'd felt to be tangled up in his arms.

"Just admit it, you're afraid of horses."

"I'm not afraid of horses," Harper insisted, hating that she couldn't just suck it up and do this ridiculous touristy zip lining without wanting to pee her pants. But as much as she wanted to tell Teagan the real reason she was shaking, she held it in. Showing weakness wasn't something she did. "Fear is the mind killer," she whispered to herself, surprised when Teagan heard her.

"Dune?"

She opened her eyes, surprised. "You've seen *Dune*?"

"Yeah, it's a classic. Kyle MacLachlan as Muad'Dib, hell yes. Love it. One of my favorites."

She resisted being charmed that he enjoyed the same cult classic as she did but what were the odds?

"I like sci-fi and fantasy flicks," Harper admitted, joking wryly. "If I'd been better at science…who knows what I might've become."

"Me, too." He laughed and she secretly smiled.

They shared favorite movies and it helped lessen her growing panic until they reached their destination. The base was situated around one of the largest trees with a platform and the rigging. Just seeing how far she'd have to climb to get up there made her shake.

The mule whinnied and shuffled at the sudden tension in her thighs and Teagan patted the animal's neck, soothing him with soft words.

Maybe he could pat her on the head and work the same magic.

"Do you need help climbing down?" he asked.

She shook her head, distrustful that her voice wouldn't shake, and carefully dismounted to stand on rubber legs.

And her vagina felt as if she'd done one too many spin classes on a bicycle seat made of cement.

No wonder cowboys were bowlegged.

Harper stretched, wincing as she worked out the kinks, not only from the mule but last night's shenanigans, and tried not to pay too much attention to Teagan when she was sorely tempted to run into the cove of his arms and hide there.

If Teagan noticed she was on edge, he didn't call her on it and she was grateful, but when she hung back to the end of the line, he stayed with her, making small talk for her benefit.

One by one, the adventurers suited up and went squealing over the jungle canopy like crazed featherless kamikaze birds—including Vanessa and Stuart—until it was only Teagan and Harper remaining.

"Ready?" he asked, extending his hand after they were suited up. She stood stock-still, helmet jammed on her head and safety rigging crisscrossing her body as they prepared to hook her carabiner to the line. "Harper?"

But she froze. "I can't." *Oh, God*, here was the moment she'd dreaded. Either she was going to pee or faint. She wasn't sure which would be worse. "I just can't."

Teagan realized she wasn't joking or playing around and his demeanor changed, going instantly from athletic adrenaline junkie to concerned gentleman in the blink of an eye. "What's wrong?" he asked.

"I'm afraid of heights," she blurted to her shame. Tears immediately followed. "I can't do it. I'm afraid I'll be the one person who dies on a zip line. I'll be the one percent that no one talks about."

She was becoming hysterical but she was past the point of caring. Her lungs felt ready to seize. She couldn't draw a deep breath. Harper fluttered her hands as panic began crowding her ability to remain calm. "I—I—I can't b-breathe…"

The tour guide tried to assure her it was safe but Harper couldn't hear him any longer.

Teagan gently gripped her shoulders and caught her gaze. "It's okay," he said. "You can do this. I will be right here. You won't be alone. If it turns out you're the one percent, I'll go down with you. We'll face it together."

She slowed her breathing and stared at Teagan. "You would?"

"Of course, I would."

"I still don't want to go," Harper admitted in a small voice. "Do I have to go?"

The tour guide chimed in, worried, "Si, the mules are already gone up the trail back to the saddle master. This way is the only way back to the bus."

Harper groaned. This couldn't be happening. "I'll pay you extra if you get me back to the bus without going down that death line," she pleaded with the man.

"Sorry, this the only way. It quick, though." He gestured with a silly grin as if that would encourage Harper to ditch her fears and hop on.

Teagan caught her chin and dragged her attention back to him. "I will hold your hand the whole way."

Harper cast her gaze toward the double zip lines and realized that she and Teagan would be side by side. Knowing he would be there where she could see him made the panic lessen but she still didn't want to do it.

But Harper knew with a sinking heart that going down that line was the only way she was returning to their ship.

And that meant swallowing the golf-ball-sized lump in her throat, praying to God and going for it.

"Fine," she said tightly, inching her way to the push-off

point as the guide locked the carabiners in place. "But if I die, I'm so coming back as a vengeful spirit and haunting every single person, including you, Juan!"

The tour guide blanched and crossed himself as if afraid that her curse might hold some weight and then, gripping Teagan's hand in a death clutch, they were airborne before she could even manage a scream.

The wind whistled through her hair and cooled the nervous sweat covering her body. She tentatively opened her eyes and saw the true, untouched beauty beneath her. It was wild, untamed and dangerous but incredibly serene, as well.

Her fear slowly loosened and gave way to wonder and by the time they bounced to a stop at the end platform, Harper was grinning in spite of the fact her heart was pounding so hard, it hurt.

Vanessa and Stuart clapped as they arrived, sending up a supportive "Good job!" followed by "Wasn't that fun?" and Harper laughed weakly as she nodded.

It was then she realized she was still holding Teagan's hand as if her life depended on it.

She unfurled her fingers and saw the crescent moons carved into his palm from her nails and bit her lip. "Sorry," Harper offered as they climbed out of their rigging. "I didn't mean to—"

"No worries," Teagan said, his gaze warm enough to bask in for a heartbeat. The genuine compassion in his eyes was more than she could handle. But before it could get awkward, Teagan turned to Stuart and clapped him heartily on the shoulder. "Mark that sucker off your bucket list," he declared with a wide grin and Stuart nodded vigorously.

"That felt good. Real good. I can't believe I've never done that before. What's next?" he asked Vanessa, giddy as a schoolboy.

"Next is a cool, frothy drink with an umbrella in it," Vanessa answered with a wink.

It was damn near impossible to ignore the fact that Stuart and Vanessa had a real connection when she was struggling to create some kind of false one.

The real connection she had was with the man she needed to stay away from.

So instead of letting Vanessa and Stuart have their moment, Harper stepped away from Teagan and said brightly, "I'd love a drink. Count me in."

She may have turned away from Teagan but it wasn't fast enough to avoid seeing his disappointment.

Why his opinion weighed on her conscience was another troubling matter.

For now, she needed to find a way to get Teagan out of her mind and Vanessa out of Stuart's.

The problem?

The thought left her cold on both fronts.

_15_

TEAGAN SHOULDN'T HAVE been disappointed, but the minute Harper went from him to Stuart within a blink, inserting herself in what was clearly an invitation for two, was hard to ignore.

His disgust rose and he stalked away, walking to the bus alone. If Harper noticed—or cared—she certainly didn't show it.

Ten minutes later, the rest of the group arrived at the bus and filed in. Just as before, the quarters were close and although he wasn't excited about sitting next to Harper, there simply wasn't enough space to be choosy.

She settled in beside him and he chose to look out the window, effectively shutting her out.

Harper broke the silence first. "So we're going to get a drink at Senior Frog's when we get back to town. Want to come?"

"I think one third wheel is plenty, don't you think?" he answered coolly without breaking his gaze from the dusty window.

"What's that supposed to mean?" she asked.

"Playing dumb is beneath you."

"I don't know what you're talking about. Vanessa mentioned wanting a drink and I thought it was a great idea. I don't know if you caught this or not, but doing that zip line thing was a big deal for me. I think I've earned something cold and frosty."

She was really going to play like she hadn't purposefully inserted herself where she wasn't invited? The balls on Harper were bigger than his. Fine. She wanted to play games? He'd play.

"Yeah? So you're just in it for the drink? Not to wedge yourself between two people who seem to be hitting it off? Forgive me, but it seemed a little desperate to me."

Her cheeks colored. "That's a mean thing to say."

"But true?" he countered, shaking his head. "When are you going to learn that screwing people over isn't going to win you any points in the end."

"The end of what?"

"Life, baby. Everyone has to answer to someone."

She rolled her eyes. "Now you're a philosopher?"

He ignored her dig and put her on the spot just to see how far she'd take it. "Okay, you say you're in it for a celebratory drink... I'm down. Let's leave the two people who are getting along great to themselves and we'll find someplace else to find a cold one."

"But shouldn't we stay with the group?" she said, faltering. "I mean, for safety purposes?"

"This isn't my first time in Mexico. I'll keep you safe if that's what you're worried about."

"I just think we should stay together," Harper said, obviously unable to think of a better argument, not that it would've mattered. Teagan knew it was all a bunch of horseshit, anyway. Harper was determined to steal Stuart away from a woman who really seemed to like him, and vice versa, because Harper needed a payday.

Goddamn. He was pissed off.

Why did he care so much what Harper did with her life?

Teagan wasn't trying to be the knight in shining armor. They were all adults on this cruise. If Stuart allowed himself to be swayed by someone like Harper when he had a good woman on his arm already, what business was it of his to interfere?

Hell, he didn't know, but he was having a hard time swallowing his decision to leave Harper in the dust.

Was it the sex? Pretty damn good sex. But still, he was old enough to know that centering an entire relationship on what goes on between the sheets was a recipe for disaster.

So why couldn't he just walk?

Even mad as a wet hornet, he still wanted her.

Correction, he wanted Harper to give up this insane plan of hers and spend time with him because she wanted to, not because he had a fat bank account.

His bank account wasn't anemic by any means but—let's get real—he was no Stuart Buck.

"Are you going to be mad at me all night?" Harper surprised him by asking.

"And why would I be mad?" he returned quietly, afraid he might start yelling his fool head off in front of all the nice people on the bus. "I don't care what you do with your life."

"I just wanted a goddamn drink! Why are you being such a prick?"

That was it. Final straw. He turned and gripped her chin, drawing her close so that only she could hear his words.

"Just back off from Stuart. Find another target for your payday. He's a good man and he doesn't deserve to be sucked dry by someone like you. Vanessa is a better match for him and you know it."

He released her and caught the shine of sudden tears in her eyes but he wasn't swayed. A woman like Harper could probably produce the waterworks on command.

Okay, maybe he was a little swayed—he wasn't a jerk— but he told himself it was likely an act. Harper had been pretty clear about what she wanted from him and what she didn't want.

It was all about the sex.

He closed his eyes and drew a deep breath.

If sex was all she wanted, then Teagan would oblige her.

It wasn't a huge tragedy to screw Harper six ways from Sunday.

Maybe he'd been overthinking things, anyway.

Sex—epic sex, at that—wasn't meant for the long haul. Anything that burned that hot burned out quickly.

Maybe Harper was doing him a favor by keeping things superficial between them.

The last thing he needed was to get emotionally tangled up with a woman like Harper. He could only imagine how many notches she had on her bedpost from men she'd eaten alive.

Yeah, well, it was one thing to try and convince yourself of something when you're mad, quite another when you've sobered from your bruised ego and realize that, crap, feelings are involved, after all.

He wanted Harper.

How was it his dumb luck that he'd have to find the one woman on the entire ship who couldn't be more wrong for him?

The bus pulled to a stop in town where they'd boarded and everyone dispersed in different directions. It didn't escape his notice that Vanessa and Stuart had snuck off, taking matters into their own hands without making things awkward, leaving Harper and Teagan by themselves again.

"You still want that drink?" he asked.

Harper cut him a reproachful look. "With you? Certainly not."

"Suit yourself. You might want to head back to the ship, then. The streets aren't safe for a single young woman."

"I can take care of myself."

He tipped an imaginary hat toward her and then started walking away in the direction of a bar he knew. He needed a beer and didn't want to pay an arm and a leg for it like he would on the ship.

Suddenly, the sound of feet running after him made him smile with knowing. Little Miss I Can Take Care Of Myself wasn't so sure about being alone.

"Change your mind?"

"Shut up and just buy me a drink," she grumbled as they walked into the small bar.

Teagan liked the bar because it wasn't a tourist trap, but then, it wasn't fancy, either. It was a place the locals enjoyed, which meant the drinks were stiff and the bartender wasn't going to rob them blind.

They grabbed a couple stools at the bar and Teagan ordered two beers.

Once two cold ones were delivered, Teagan took the time to savor that first drink, letting everything else slide away for the moment.

A good beer could save a bad moment.

At least, most times.

Teagan wasn't sure a beer was strong enough to handle the storm building inside him for no good reason.

All he knew was that he wanted to shake some sense into Harper before she irreparably damaged something good in two people's lives.

TEAGAN'S JUDGMENT SAT heavily on Harper's shoulders.

Why did she care what he thought of her plan or how she lived her life?

The breadth of his broad shoulders were just the perfect size to rest her head on but he looked as cuddly as a sea urchin at the moment.

"Why are you so mad at me?" she asked, a bit defensive. "It's not as if we're a thing. I told you from the start—me and you—just isn't going to work."

"Honey, I heard you loud and clear. Not asking to marry you," he muttered, his attention centered on enjoying his beer. After a good swallow, he added, "Look, you can do what you want, but I'm not going to sit and watch you self-

ishly put your interests before everyone else's. In case you're
blind, Stuart is really into Vanessa. Hard pill to swallow,
isn't it, Hot Stuff? Must be difficult to realize that you're
not irresistible."

Why did he have to make her feel small like that?

"Ask me why I have to do what I'm doing," she said.

He cut her a sharp look. "I don't care. Nothing can justify
what you're doing."

Frustration ate at her for a couple reasons: one, for caring
about his opinion and two, because he was right.

Now she wanted to cry.

It was the overall rush of adrenaline, she reasoned. De-
fying death and all that. Normal reaction. Drawing a deep
breath, she ignored Teagan for the moment and sipped her
beer to collect herself.

Mmm, it's good, at the very least.

"How nice for you that you've lived a perfect life,"
Harper said. "Not everyone is as lucky."

"What makes you think I've lived a perfect life?" Teagan asked with a scowl. "Honey, just because I don't make
it my business to stomp on other people doesn't mean I
haven't been given my share of screws in the life depart-
ment. Think of this…maybe you didn't corner the market
on pain."

Harper opened her mouth to defend herself but he had
other plans and kept going, gaining steam as he went.

"I've watched fellow airmen die in the line of duty.
I've attended funerals for soldiers who took their own
life when the PTSD got to be too much to handle. I've
chased my little brother all around the world, trying to
keep his ass alive, and most recently, had my entire life
blown up, including my business, when my brother got
tangled up with a lunatic billionaire drug lord. I've slept
on the ground with nothing but leaves to cover me, I've
eaten bugs to survive, hell, I've even done things I can't
talk about because they're classified but that don't mean

they don't haunt me at night. So, yeah, baby girl, we all got pain. How you deal with it is the measure of your character." He cast her a dismissive glance. "So far, your character sucks."

Why didn't she get up and leave him there? At the very least tell him to stick his judgment up his ass and spin on it?

Because she couldn't speak.

The lump in her throat was too tight, blocking her airway and choking off her ability to speak.

No. Stop. He doesn't have the right to shame you for your choices.

That tiny voice of defiance was the one thing keeping her from openly bawling.

Her heart rate quickened as she struggled with her need to cry, scream or flat out tell him to mind his own business.

But after a few gulped breaths, she regained her composure, finished her beer and tossed a few dollars on the bar, saying as she rose to leave, "I wouldn't want you to think I was using you for your money."

At that, he quirked that annoyingly handsome grin and said, "Baby, no worries there. I know you're just using me for sex and I'm good with that."

Her cheeks flared with heat as a few people glanced their way and she hustled from the bar, eager to escape the unwelcome feelings cramming their way down her throat.

She had to return to her room. Decompress. Get focused.

Or maybe Harper would just cry her eyes out in her own pity party for one.

No one understood the struggle.

The loneliness.

The yawning chasm of emptiness that grew with each passing year as she chased her goal.

She just wanted to be self-sufficient, never beholden to anyone.

Ever.

The only way to get there was the path laid out for her.

Damn you, Teagan Carmichael—you don't get to judge me.

Only God can judge me and so far, He hasn't seen fit to say a word.

So cram it, asshole.

16

IN HINDSIGHT, MAYBE he should've cut himself off at the third beer.

Or the tequila shot.

Or even the whiskey body shot off the soft belly of that hot local woman.

But he hadn't.

Which was probably why he didn't quite remember how he got the black eye he was sporting.

Gotta love Mexico.

At least his wallet was still in his pocket.

Teagan might not remember how he got back to the ship or what exactly happened after Harper left, but he did remember in excruciating detail how crushed she'd looked, even if she'd tried to hide it.

He'd hurt her.

Teagan rubbed his head, the angry pain of a killer hangover bludgeoning his brain, and rose to guzzle some water and eat some aspirin for breakfast.

He didn't know why he couldn't just let Harper do what she planned to do. It really wasn't his business how she ran her life.

But he did care.

Damn, he cared a lot.

More than he wanted to.

Harper was more than she sold herself as and it pissed him off that she was chasing after a plan that stank of deception and lies.

Teagan wanted to grab her by the shoulders and shake some sense into her.

But if he put his hands on her…he couldn't promise that he wouldn't go a step further and just screw the sense into her.

He chuckled at his own stupidity. *Yeah, like that's possible.* If it were, their epic first night together would've accomplished far more than it had.

Teagan grabbed a bottled water and washed the aspirin down, catching a brief look at his sorry self in the bathroom mirror before walking away in disgust.

It'd been quite a while since he'd thrown punches in a bar.

He liked to think he'd outgrown that bullshit.

Apparently not.

A knock at the door made his head throb anew.

When he saw Vanessa holding an ice pack, he swallowed his disappointment that it wasn't Harper and let her in.

"Sorry, not the right gal you were hoping for?" Vanessa said, winking.

He needed to work on his game face. "Sorry," he said, sheepish as he fell back onto the small sofa with a groan. "Do you have any idea what happened to me? Or how I got back to my room?"

"Yes and yes," Vanessa answered, handing him the ice. "Figured you might need this."

"Yeah, I do. Thanks," he said, placing the ice on his forehead. "I feel like I went a few rounds with Mike Tyson and lost."

"You didn't win," Vanessa agreed with a short laugh. "But you gave it a good college try. To be fair, the numbers weren't in your favor."

That caught his attention, and he removed the ice pack. "What do you mean?"

"The thing about local bars is that they usually have locals in them," Vanessa answered as if that should be obvious. "And locals hate tourists."

"I've been to that bar before and never had a problem."

"Yeah, but you have that look about you on this trip that screams 'I'm not from here' and well, you've also got a face that can make other men instantly jealous. Pretty boy problems."

"Pretty boy? Not sure anyone has ever called me that." He replaced the ice. "And with this shiner, I doubt they will anytime soon."

"All right, well, let me give you the short version of what happened."

"Please do. I'm all ears."

Vanessa took a seat opposite him. "Me and Stuart finished up our drink and started to head back to the ship. We happened to pass Harper and she looked upset so we tried to ask her what was wrong and she gave us some vague total baloney answer, which we saw right through, and then because we knew that you two had left together, we asked where you were. She told us, and then split. We got to the bar just in time to see you taking a punch. Judging by the general mayhem, it looked as if you got a few lucky strikes in but, honey, you have to know when you're outnumbered."

"I don't remember any of that. I remember Harper leaving, but…after that… I kinda drank more than I usually do."

"Something tells me that young thing could drive any man to drink," Vanessa joked, amused by the entire situation when she should be outraged that Harper had sights on Stuart. He didn't understand women. "The only reason you weren't arrested and thrown into a Mexican jail was because Stuart made the problems go away."

"How?" he asked.

"Money," she answered simply. "That man is generous

to a fault, which is why you need to get off your ass and stop playing footsie with Harper."

"Trust me, not playing anything with her."

"That's the problem."

He did a double take. "Come again?"

"Look, honey, I know Harper thinks she's going to put her baby claws in Stuart and I know why she's so keen on getting him, but she needs to know that I'm not going to let that happen and I'd rather not crush the poor girl for her ambition. I like her," Vanessa admitted with a shrug. "She has spunk."

"Yeah, well, Harper has her mind set. Not sure there's much else I can do to change that."

Vanessa waved away Teagan's sour attitude. "You have to be dumber than a box of rocks if you can't see that girl is into you. Like *really* into you. She can hardly take her eyes off you and when you two are together, that sexual tension is contagious."

Couldn't argue the point about the tension. Even when he was pissed as hell, he still wanted to feel her beneath him.

It felt a little weird to be talking about this with Vanessa.

But Vanessa got a kick out of it, apparently.

"And to think, I thought *you* were going to be my catch on this trip. Fate is funny. Now I'm glad I wasn't your cup of tea. Stuart is…well, he's damn awesome. And virile for a man his age. Flexible, too."

Teagan tried not to look sick but the mental image of Stuart doing the Kama sutra with Vanessa was more than his brain could handle.

"You two seemed to have hit it off," Teagan said, hoping to nudge the topic to safer ground. "I'm glad. You're a helluva woman. Stuart is lucky."

"Yes, he is." Vanessa smiled widely. "But you need to get your A game in better shape because that girl is a powder keg of need and want. All it's going to take is the right spark to cause an explosion."

"She's not interested," he said, chuckling at Vanessa's assessment. "I appreciate you and Stuart keeping my dumb ass out of a Mexican jail, I really do, but I think I'm just going to keep my distance from Harper. She and I are like oil and water, they just don't mix well."

"I call it fire and ice," Vanessa corrected with a sly expression. "Look, trust me, I'm a woman. I understand the complexities of a woman's mind. You're going to have to believe me when I say she's into you a lot more than she wants to admit. It's your job to press the right buttons."

Oh, he knew the right buttons on her body to push, but the mental buttons? He couldn't seem to find the right switch.

He sighed. "Got any ideas?"

"More of what you did today," Vanessa answered promptly, already with a solution. "She was scared to death until you went on that zip with her. She trusts you. I'm willing to bet trust is something she's got in short supply. Give her more. Show her that you're not going to break her like someone did in the past. It's really not that hard to figure out, honey. Sometimes you got to get a little dirty to find the treasure buried underground."

"That's some philosophical stuff you're dropping on me," he said, half joking.

Vanessa smiled and rose, pleased with herself. "Just do as I've told you and you'll have that sassy girl eating out of your palm."

Teagan wasn't so sure about that, but he respected Vanessa enough to give her the benefit of the doubt.

Hell, maybe Vanessa was right and he really was dumb as a box of rocks for not seeing what was right in front of him.

"Now," Vanessa said, heading for the door, "shower, slap some deodorant on and meet us downstairs in an hour. We have a new excursion planned and I can't wait."

Excursion?

Vanessa wiggled her fingers in goodbye and then she was gone.

That was the thing about older women…wisdom, man, wisdom.

Hopefully, Stuart's ticker could handle all that woman.

If not, at least the old guy would die with a smile on his face.

HARPER KNEW SHE ought to get up, dress and return to the schedule, but her heart wasn't in it.

Staying locked in her suite seemed a great idea.

So did eating a bucket of ice cream—not that she would ever do that—but she could fantasize.

Munching on carrot and celery sticks didn't have the same soothing effect as a creamy sugary treat, but at least she could eat the veggies without worrying that the extra calories might end up on her behind.

When she finally made enough money to retire, she was going to eat ice cream until she puked.

And pizza.

And chocolate chip cookies.

And fettuccine Alfredo with tender bay shrimp and garlic bread.

Ohh, bread, she groaned. She missed carbs.

Something slid under the door and she sat up abruptly with a curious frown.

A neat white envelope with her name on it had been slipped into her room like something out of a spy movie.

Her first thought was of Teagan. Seemed like something he would do.

But when she started to smile at the thought, Harper stuffed it down and snatched up the envelope, ready to trash it if it was.

She opened the envelope and saw with surprise Stuart's name scrawled on the back.

Stuart had sent her an invitation to something?

Maybe her luck was turning around.

Harper read the invitation, puzzled.

"Join us for an excursion, off the book! Meet in the lobby in one hour."

Us? Off-book?

What did any of that mean?

Well, it was an invitation from Stuart, so that was a good sign. Maybe she'd prematurely lost hope that the older gentleman was interested.

Maybe whatever he and Vanessa had shared had run its course.

Or maybe…oh, screw it, whatever the reason, she was going to make the best of it.

Besides, if she was off with Stuart, she'd stop thinking about Teagan and that was most important.

Of all things, she felt this odd tug and pull, which smacked too hard of yearning to be trusted.

She couldn't actually miss Teagan.

It hadn't even been twenty-four hours since she'd left him in that bar.

And he'd been a jerk.

A *judgy* jerk at that.

But he had been incredibly wonderful with her on the zip line.

It was hard not to fall just a little bit for a guy in protector mode.

When that tug became sharper, Harper pinned her hair and climbed into the shower, determined to make the most out of this unusual opportunity and to forget all about Teagan.

At least she knew if it was another zip line adventure, she could handle it without embarrassing herself.

Eye on the prize, girl. Eye on the prize.

The mantra managed to get her ready and downstairs, but the minute she stepped foot on the deck where Stuart was waiting, she realized with a start that the group included Teagan.

Suck a duck.

Couldn't she catch a break?

Harper immediately noticed the subtle shadowing beneath Teagan's right eye and alarm followed. What had happened to Teagan's face? Had someone hit him? The need to know momentarily eclipsed her distress at being thrown together, yet again, but she managed to handle it before she embarrassed herself.

"So happy you could join us," Stuart said, grinning as he motioned for Harper to join them. "I have a special treat in store."

Forcing a smile, Harper dragged her feet to meet them. Avoiding Teagan at all costs, she looked to Stuart. "What's going on? Your invitation was a little veiled."

Vanessa took point. "Honey, we are going to do a little exploration, just the four of us. Stuart has arranged a helicopter to pick us up at port and take us to the Mayan ruins. Doesn't that sound amazing?"

It sounded incredible.

But Stuart wasn't doing it for Harper, he was doing it for Vanessa. That was plain as the nose on Harper's face.

Did she really want to spend the afternoon watching as her dreams went up in smoke?

Really, if Stuart was into Vanessa like he seemed to be, there was no point in following him around any longer.

Perhaps she could bow out gracefully, feign an illness— Ebola, maybe?

However, Vanessa was already moving forward, like the mad current in a bloated river. Before she knew it, they were hustling off the ship and going straight to their transport.

An executive helicopter awaited them at the heliport and Harper sheepishly admitted to herself, the idea of a private tour of an ancient ruin was pretty fantastic.

Teagan's eyes lit up with appreciation when he saw the

helicopter. He said with open delight, "Gorgeous piece of machinery," and climbed inside to chat with the pilot before takeoff.

Harper tried to ignore the tingle in her belly, but Teagan was damn sexy when he smiled with genuine happiness or intrigue. Made her want to grab his cheeks and put a kiss on those entirely too kissable lips.

Pulling her gaze away from Teagan, she drew a deep breath and followed Vanessa and Stuart into the helicopter.

She wasn't surprised when she saw the only open seat was next to Teagan's. Harper was beginning to suspect some amateur matchmaking at work.

Ironic.

If she weren't so pressed to find a solution, she might've found it funny.

But at the moment, laughter wasn't her go-to reaction.

Harper struggled against the urge to set Stuart and Vanessa straight about her interest in Teagan, but even as she formulated the words, she knew it would be hard to sell.

There was something about Teagan that called to her.

Last night had sucked.

Well, sleeping without him had sucked.

And that was plainly ridiculous because a) she preferred sleeping alone; and b) she'd only slept with him one night.

But the facts were hard to ignore—she'd tossed and turned all night.

Punching her pillow.

Staring at the ceiling.

Wondering if he was thinking about her.

Replaying how sweet he'd been with her.

Replaying what a jerk he'd been, too.

All those turbulent thoughts made it hard to catch a wink, which was why she could thank Teagan for the slight dark circles ringing her eyes.

They slipped headphones over their ears and the pilot

started his cheery "Hi, I'm your pilot" introduction as they lifted off.

It wasn't the first time she'd flown by helicopter but the experience never got old.

"First we're going to give you a fun, aerial view of our majestic Mexican landscape where you'll see waterfalls only accessible by foot, deep in the jungle. Then, we'll head over to one of the seven wonders of the world, Chichen Itza, where you'll get to experience the incredible mathematical genius of an ancient civilization."

A smile found Harper's lips as she peered out the window, enjoying the view.

"I thought you were afraid of heights?"

Teagan's voice in her ear sent a shiver down her arms.

She glanced at him. "As long as this helicopter remains airborne, I'll be fine."

He chuckled and she ignored the flutter of excitement tickling her insides.

It was too easy to remember that deep chuckle rumbling through her body when she was pressed tightly against him, his hands roving, his mouth tasting.

Don't go there. Stop it.

Harper drew a halting breath and returned to the scenery. Trees were good. Safe.

Teagan was not for her.

17

TEAGAN SHOULD'VE KNOWN Vanessa would throw them all together after their little chat that morning, but it was a little jarring to see Harper again after last night.

He felt like an idiot, sporting a shiner like a kid, but he'd be a liar if he didn't admit seeing Harper sent wild arcs of electricity snapping through him.

His hands fidgeted with the desire to touch.

His mouth needed to be on hers.

And if he wasn't careful, he'd be sporting a woody to go with his embarrassing black eye.

The fact that he'd gotten so blitzed last night was an indication that Harper was already under his skin.

Was fate punishing him for some crime he was unaware he'd committed?

It was true, in his youth, he'd been a little wild, but once Teagan had realized that both Carmichael brothers couldn't run around tearing things up, he became the responsible one.

At times, the boring one.

Harper reminded him that he used to be fun.

Used to enjoy getting wild.

He chuckled to himself, forgetting that Harper could hear him. She caught his gaze and he stared at her.

The things I want to do to you...

Harper's tongue wet her bottom lip and he had to hold himself back to keep from lunging at her and sucking it into his mouth.

Her cheeks bloomed and she quickly returned to her view out the window.

At least he could take comfort in knowing that he wasn't alone in his feelings.

Maybe Vanessa was right; Harper was fighting her attraction to him and he needed to push harder.

It was time to get to know the real Harper...not the sex-kitten, man-eater part she played.

The trouble was...what if Harper was afraid to show him what was beneath the mask?

If Vanessa was right, maybe it was his job to show Harper with his actions that she could trust him with all her secrets.

He didn't care about her past, what mattered was the present.

If his time in the military had taught him anything, it was to appreciate the moment.

And the moment belonged to him and Harper.

But how could he get Harper to see that, too?

He wanted to show her that he saw more than the beautiful woman.

Perhaps the key to winning Harper's trust was to ignore the physical and go deeper.

He wanted to get personal.

What was her favorite food? Did she have any family? What kind of music did she like? Turnoffs? Turn-ons? Phobias—aside from heights—and pet peeves?

Teagan wanted to know it all.

Maybe then, Harper would realize he was interested in more than her body.

It was worth a shot.

Time to show Harper that he was more than just a horny guy, interested in getting in her pants for a good romp.

If she'd let him, Teagan was willing to go all in.

SHE NEEDED AIR.

Harper's breath quickened as she felt the insides of the chopper close in on her.

Teagan was everywhere.

The scent of his skin teased her nose.

The warmth of his solid body against her side reminded her of things she needed to forget.

The rumble of his voice in her ear turned her insides to liquid.

Just as she was about to do something irrational, such as start pounding on the Plexiglas so she could jump out, the pilot announced their descent.

She wasted no time in escaping the confined space and practically leaped from her seat once the door was open.

If anyone noticed her odd behavior, no one commented because Stuart was already talking.

"We have a few hours to explore, and then we'll meet back here for a picnic lunch catered by a local eatery that will deliver, and then we'll pack up and head back to the ship."

Once Harper could breathe again, she realized why Chichen Itza was a wonder of the world.

"This is incredible," she managed to say around her gasp. "It's huge."

"And they made this all by hand," Stuart said. "The Mayans are the ancestral architects of today's modern world."

"This is incredible," Harper admitted. "And kind of... I don't know, intimidating."

Vanessa nodded in agreement. "Glad I'm visiting the ruin and not actually taking a trip back in time. Not sure I'd enjoy the Mayan way of life."

"You would probably be sacrificed to the Mayan Gods for your exotic beauty," Stuart teased, and Vanessa swiped at him playfully.

Harper was too amazed by the ruins to take more than

a cursory notice of Stuart and Vanessa's cozy canoodling. She wanted to care but at the moment, she simply didn't. The ruins had completely captured her attention.

The rock-hewn steps leading to the top of Temple of *Kukulcan*, or El Castillo as it was known, were protected with limited access but that was okay, because Harper was astounded simply by seeing it from the ground.

Vanessa and Stuart went hand in hand to go explore with the help of a travel book Vanessa had picked up and they were soon off doing their own thing, leaving Teagan and Harper alone.

Again.

This time, Harper noticed. "They are doing this on purpose," Harper said with a faint frown. "We really need to set them straight."

"Someone needs to be set straight," he agreed, slipping his hand into hers before she could stop him. "C'mon, let's explore."

She should've tugged her hand free but it felt good to have his hand wrapped around hers. It was silly, but she felt incredibly safe around Teagan.

Emotional safety hadn't been a luxury she could afford.

In spite of being one of the top visited places in Mexico, the crowds were thin and easily navigated as they walked around the ruins.

She'd never been particularly religious or spiritual, but it was hard to ignore the dense heaviness in the air, as if the ghosts of the past were still hanging around.

"You okay?" Teagan asked when he caught her rubbing the goose bumps from her arms.

"I know it sounds stupid, but…this place has a lot of weird energy. Either that, or it's the humidity messing with my hair and my brain."

She expected him to laugh or poke fun at her but he didn't. Instead, he said, "I've seen too many things in my life that I can't explain to make quick judgments about anything. The Mayans, for all their intelligence, were a brutal race. Lots of human sacrifice going on. I wouldn't doubt there's some residual energy floating around."

"Really?" Harper said, smiling shyly at Teagan for not making her feel stupid. "Yeah, that makes sense."

"Besides, it's hard to ignore the fact that the Mayans seemed to know things they couldn't possibly have understood given their limited technology. Either it's supernatural or...aliens."

Harper laughed. "Aliens?"

"Yeah, what else makes sense?"

He was joking but he was semiserious, too. That made her laugh harder.

"Hey, if you can believe in ghosts, I can believe in aliens," he said with mock affront.

"You're absolutely right," Harper said, shaking her head in apology. "Who knows, maybe it was aliens."

"Exactly."

"All right, you were in the military—did some secret missions—is Area 51 where they really keep the alien bodies?"

Teagan sobered. "If I told you, I'd have to kill you. Classified."

Harper laughed, enjoying their banter so much she didn't even resist when Teagan pulled her in for a kiss.

It seemed so natural and so right to be wrapped in his arms, the sun bathing them in golden light, that she sank into his kiss, loving the way he pulled her close and held her as if she were his greatest treasure.

This was what a true courtship was supposed to feel like—heady and intoxicating—not calculated or manipulated.

"What am I going to do with you?" she murmured against his lips, fighting the smile.

"Whatever comes natural," he suggested, but they both knew what they wanted and it had nothing to do with walking around the ruins. The moment grew dense between them until it seemed they were the only two people on the planet. Her clothes scratched against her warmed skin, as if encouraging her to do something reckless.

"Too bad we aren't alone," he said, dragging reality back into play. They were surrounded by people who, no doubt, wouldn't appreciate an X-rated show while on vacation. Teagan slowly let her go but the promise in his eyes remained. Sliding his hand back in hers, he said, "Let's check out this creepy cool place so we can at least say we've seen it."

She laughed with a shaky nod. "Lead the way. I'm terrible at direction."

"Lucky for you, I know exactly where I'm going."

It sounded like a double entendre—it probably was—but Harper didn't care. The giddy bubbles in her stomach were too enjoyable to stomp out.

What was one more night in the big scheme of things?

This trip was a bust. Might as well enjoy some quality sex while she was nursing her ego.

And she couldn't imagine anyone she'd rather work out those tensions with than Teagan Carmichael.

18

HAND IN HAND, Teagan and Harper explored the ancient city, laughing and even cracking a few jokes as they marveled at the architecture and artistic expression carved from the stones.

"Everything is so masculine," she noted, peering at the menacing open mouth of the snake carved into the base of the staircase. "I don't see anything that I would attribute to a female influence."

"Not surprising for a people who engaged in ritual sacrifice of their enemies and sometimes children," Teagan said.

"Children?" Harper repeated, aghast. "How awful."

"In times of drought they often threw treasured objects into the Cenote Sagrado for the god Chac in the hopes of pleasing him. I can't imagine anything more treasured than their kids," Teagan said.

"How do you know all this? Are you an archeologist in your spare time?"

Teagan produced a small pamphlet from his back pocket with a grin. "I snagged this at the entrance. It's pretty interesting. Filled with good info."

Harper laughed. "And here I thought you were just really smart."

"I have my moments but my Mayan history is a little rusty."

Harper pulled the pamphlet from his hand and started reading, her brow furrowing as she skimmed the information. "Should we go see the sacrificial waters?" she asked, sending him a cheeky smile for using the brochure's verbiage. "Sounds like a cheery place."

Teagan grasped her hand and tugged her close. "Or we could find a secluded spot and invoke the ancient gods' favor with a fertility rite," he suggested with a dirty grin.

She gasped as his hand found her rounded behind. "Oh, my God, Teagan," she squeaked with an adorable blush. "Someone could see us."

"I don't care," he said, sealing his mouth to hers in a firm kiss. His tongue found hers and she didn't hold back in spite of her supposed protests. She was taking as much as she was giving. It didn't take long before he was near busting out of his shorts. Teagan reluctantly ended the kiss, pleased to see her lids at half-mast and her lips reddened and plump. His libido was on overdrive but he managed to throttle down, determined to show Harper that he was into more than just sex with her. "Okay," he said roughly, "let's find this pool of death."

Harper laughed and followed his lead, her sunny smile lighting up his insides.

They arrived at the Cenote Sagrado and Harper was relieved to see it was roped off.

"Thank God," she said, peering past the roped-off section to the giant, gaping maw of the cenote. "I can't imagine being tossed into that thing to drown. How awful."

The cenote was nearly perfectly round with a layer of brilliant green muck covering the surface.

The fresh water bubbled up from deep in the earth but there was little to move the water around, so the top seemed to stagnate a bit.

"And they threw kids into this thing?" Harper asked, appalled. "It's pretty awful."

"Different cultures," Teagan reminded her. "And it was, like, hundreds upon hundreds of years ago. It's not as if they could Google better ways to appease their gods. They were doing what they thought was best."

"Still awful."

The vista was quiet. Most of the tourists had vacated the cenote and moved on to other points of interest, leaving Teagan and Harper alone.

The jungle crowded around them, reminding Teagan of when he'd flown into Mexico to rescue his brother and Hope.

He supposed there was a rugged beauty about the Mexican jungle but he was less enamored of it than he had been before that near-death experience.

"You okay?" Harper asked when he quieted. "Is something wrong?"

"Big, green, leafy jungles tend to make my skin crawl."

"Why?"

"My younger brother nearly died in a Mexican jungle. The memory is hard to forget. Especially since it only happened a few months ago."

"Are you being serious? Or joking?"

If only he were joking. "It happened. But I guess it all worked out in the end. I don't know why I'm still skittish about it."

"Why did you take a Mexican cruise if you're scared of the jungle?"

"I didn't say I was scared," Teagan corrected with mock machismo. "I just said I was skittish. And I didn't book this cruise, my brother did. I think, in his own messed-up way, he was trying to blot out what'd happened before with new memories."

"How's that working out for you?"

"So far so good," he admitted, glancing around the jungle canopy. "Being here with you doesn't suck."

She laughed. "High praise, indeed."

"Hey, just being honest." He kissed her again. "Want to disappear behind those bushes and get primal?"

"You're asking me if I want to get naked with you in the jungle?" she asked, incredulous, then answered with a playful sniff. "I'm not that kind of girl."

"Oh, I know what kind of girl you *were*, Little Miss Designer Dress." Teagan slid his hand around the back of her neck to draw her to him. "But I'm more interested in the kind of woman you can *be* with *me*."

Harper gasped and he captured her mouth again, drinking in her taste and reveling in the way her body melded to his almost perfectly.

Her muffled laughter was all he needed as he carried her into a secluded area off the beaten path, like a caveman about to stake his claim.

Teagan laid her down gently and quickly freed himself from his shorts. "I want to thank you for wearing that beautiful dress," he said with a hungry smile, lifting the hem to reveal that sweet feminine place. "I'm a fan of easy access."

"Stop talking and just do me already," she demanded with an equally hungry expression. With a directive like that, how could he refuse? Teagan wasted no time in easing his length inside her hot sheath, the smell of crushed grass mixing with the jungle loving. Her legs wrapped around his torso as he drove into her, losing himself in the overwhelming pleasure of nailing Harper to the moist ground. She clutched at his back desperately, thrusting her hips against him, meeting him stroke for stroke as if she couldn't quite help herself.

"Insatiable little diva," he said, grinning as sweat began to cover their bodies. Teagan wanted to draw out the pleasure as long as possible but his body was not on board.

And apparently neither was Harper's.

She stiffened and cried out, mindless to the fact that jungle foliage was a terrible sound barrier, and Teagan followed seconds later, shouting his own release as he poured into her, jetting into her canal with desperate, hard thrusts.

If he could brand his scent onto her body, he would.

That was how primal she made him feel.

Teagan wasn't usually the type to go all caveman but with Harper, it seemed his only speed.

They both stiffened in alarm as voices approached. Withdrawing quickly, he tucked himself back into his shorts while Harper adjusted her hem and brushed off the stray leaves and dirt clinging to her hair. Teagan plucked a green fuzzy thing from her hair and they emerged from their hidden spot before more tourists arrived.

They barely held in their laughter as they escaped the curious stares of total strangers, practically running from the cenote.

They managed to reach the Temple of the Warriors before stopping to gasp for breath.

"I can't believe we did that," Harper exclaimed, laughing as she tried to breathe. "That had to be sacrilegious or something. What if we're cursed by some Mayan god for defiling his temple?"

"Something tells me the Mayan gods were good with sex. Maybe we even paid homage. Maybe we'll be blessed instead of cursed."

"Do you always manage to put a positive spin on things?" she asked, smiling.

"Don't always succeed, but I give it a good college try."

"Why are you so…"

The look of wonder and frustration sobered him. "Why am I so what?" he pressed.

"So amazing," she finished, but her tone didn't make it sound like a compliment.

"Why are you so damn stubborn?" he challenged

softly, the moment becoming as fragile as a soap bubble on the wind.

"Because that's how I've had to be."

Teagan lifted her palm to his lips. "Not anymore," he told her. "Whatever happened in the past…isn't what has to happen in the future."

For a brief, heart-stopping moment, Teagan saw the flash of hope but it dimmed as quickly as if someone had thrown water on it. She pulled her hand free with a short, pained smile, saying, "Pretty promises are easy to make but hard to keep."

And that was all she was going to say.

So much for just enjoying the moment.

How could things be so great one minute and the next, fall apart?

Harper had never felt so out of control of her own feelings than when she was with Teagan.

And that lack of control scared the crap out of her.

Her mother's DNA was contaminating her thought process.

Love wasn't real. Men didn't stay.

Get the goods while the getting's good, those were words to live by.

Not this flimsy, chemical-based attraction that was bound to fade after a few months, leaving her in a worse position than she was when she'd started.

But Teagan managed to get under her skin every time and twist up her logic.

When she was with him, everything she'd ever wanted or secretly dreamed about seemed possible.

And that was the dangerous thing.

Dreams were simply that—fluffy, ephemeral, cotton-ball clouds that evaporated under the heat of real life.

She needed a minute to get her head back on, but Teagan wasn't going to let her have a blessed minute to herself.

It was as if he knew she was on the edge but he wanted her to fall.

Was he going to catch her when she fell flat on her face?

Like Rex had promised to be there for her mom before he robbed them blind and left them destitute?

Pretty lies.

Not gonna get sucked in.

"Hold up," Teagan called out, but Harper didn't stop. She wanted to find the helicopter and hightail it out of there. Sure, that was irrational, but right now, she wasn't thinking clearly. That much was obvious because she desperately wanted to ignore her brain and simply give Teagan a chance to break her damn heart.

But Teagan picked up the pace when he realized she was trying to ditch him and quickly caught up, grasping her arm and forcing her to skid to a stop.

"What's wrong?" he asked.

He had to ask? Wasn't it obvious? But Harper didn't have it in her to explain, because if she tried, even to her own ears it would sound ridiculous and she might break down in tiny pieces.

"Teagan, I need a little space," she said, shaking her head when he tried to reach for her. "This is moving way too fast in a direction that I'm not prepared to go."

"Bullshit."

His bald statement took her back. "Excuse me?"

"I call total and complete bullshit. You're scared of feeling something with me. Why don't you just tell me what you're running from so I can help you get through it."

Damn him for being uncannily observant when it came to her private feelings. "Don't flatter yourself," she said, trying to sound like the rational one. "I don't want to hurt your feelings, but I'm trying to be honest. I'm not into you like that."

"No. I don't buy it. You're real good at putting up walls but you suck at seeing what's right in front of you."

Harper tried to chuckle with derision but it came out sounding weak and desperate…probably because she was flirting with the edge of both.

"Teagan, I—"

He silenced her with a searing kiss that immediately made her knees weak. She clutched at him for support and he pulled her close, ravaging her lips as if to both punish and arouse.

And it was working.

A needy yearning curled in her belly as wetness trickled down her leg. They hadn't used a condom. Pregnancy wasn't a concern, but cleaning up had been the last thing on her mind as they'd dashed away from the cenote.

She gasped as Teagan reached under her dress to rub the wetness around her mound, effectively smearing his seed into her skin. It should've disgusted her—but oh, God, it was the hottest thing she'd ever experienced.

It should've mattered that anyone could've noticed but Harper's thundering heartbeat blotted out all sense of propriety.

"You can fight it all you want, but you're mine," he told her, his eyes burning into her. She lost her ability to protest or even speak. "This right *here*—" he slipped a finger between her slick folds to pinch her swollen clit "—belongs to me. You and I both know it but I'm the only one willing to ride that wild wave all the way to the shore."

Harper shuddered as a second, sweet orgasm rippled through her, punctuating his words as if they had some power over her body.

She gasped, squeezing her eyes shut as waves of pleasure rolled over her, forcing Harper to hold on to Teagan or fall to the ground.

She did belong to Teagan—in her heart of hearts, she knew he was right—but there was no future between them.

Nothing worth putting her entire life on the line for.

Not even the most amazing sex in the world could make

her forget how easily her mom had been discarded and left penniless.

That would never be her.

Love was a luxury she'd long since accepted was never going to be hers.

Teagan was just going to have to accept it, too.

19

HARPER REMAINED QUIET the rest of the trip back to the ship. She smiled at the appropriate times, chatted when spoken to, but otherwise remained buttoned up.

The woman was a hard nut to crack.

He could see right through the facade she put up for everyone else's benefit and it baffled him why she was so resistant to giving him a chance.

Clearly, someone had broken her heart.

He could show her that he wasn't that guy—if she would let him.

But that was the difficult part. Harper was adamant that she wasn't going to let him see anything beyond the surface.

Teagan knew from experience, the pain from the past never healed if the person didn't allow themselves to feel.

You gotta feel to heal.

He couldn't take credit for that pithy saying. It had been said to him after a brutal mission had left him suffering from nightmares.

His therapist had walked him through some tough times.

PTSD was no joke.

He'd been open to therapy, but some of his fellow airmen…not so much.

Not everyone came out of that situation intact.

Maybe Harper had something similar to a soldier's PTSD.

Something had scarred her so much at a critical age that it'd formed a permanent scar.

If he could find out what that was…maybe he'd have a chance.

He'd stopped asking himself why he kept trying.

Unlike Harper, Teagan was ready to admit that she was the one for him.

The stubborn, difficult, manipulative little money badger was the woman he wanted above all else.

Good job, asshole.

He could just hear J.T.'s voice already.

I wanted you to get laid, not find the woman you want to marry someday.

Ha. Marriage.

Teagan had never considered himself the marrying type. He loved women but he enjoyed his freedom, too.

Now that Harper had entered the picture, he couldn't imagine wanting anyone else.

He supposed this was what'd happened to J.T. when he'd met Hope.

The hot redhead scientist had nearly gotten J.T. killed.

Several times.

And yet, J.T. couldn't seem to get enough of her.

I get it, brother. I totally get it now.

He supposed he could count his blessings that Harper didn't have bullets following her like Hope had.

But in a way, dodging a visible threat was easier than fighting an enemy that only existed in someone's mind.

How the hell was he going to prove to Harper that he wasn't like the man who'd hurt her before?

Just tie her to the bed and screw her senseless.

The thought made him smile, even if it wasn't a long-term solution.

Harper was a leaf in the wind. She came with no roots and only made surface-deep connections.

There had to be a reason she'd targeted Stuart. By all accounts, Stuart was the least like someone who would tolerate a gold digger. He wasn't swayed by her looks, or her charm. He was a genuine nice guy. Married for a lifetime to the same woman and had grieved that loss like a man who'd truly lost the love of his life.

So why would she go after Stuart instead of some greasy blowhard who was more interested in pretty arm candy than a true partner?

Lifestyles were hard to maintain without a steady flow of cash.

Did she have a spending problem? Was she already broke and needed a fatter fish to satisfy her appetite for the finer things?

Something told him that wasn't the case.

Harper was hiding more than a broken heart, he realized.

Did she have a kid to care for?

Would that matter to him?

He gauged his gut reaction to the possibility of that news. *Nope. Don't care.*

She could have a passel of kids and he'd still want her.

Maybe she was mired in credit card debt?

Not a hard theory to float given her taste.

So what, debt is a part of life these days.

Maybe she had a crazy ex in prison?

That's what restraining orders and concealed carry laws are for.

No matter what potential landmine he lobbed out there, nothing could shake his determination to have Harper as his own.

All right, so the facts were facts—he wasn't going anywhere until Harper came clean about whatever she was trying to hide.

That was the only way he'd ever have a chance to show her that he was different.

HARPER BAILED FROM the helicopter and hustled back to the ship. She didn't want to talk to anyone, least of all Teagan, before she could decompress.

Too much had happened.

She wasn't talking about the physical stuff—sex she could handle—she was talking about the mental stuff tripping her up.

Teagan was a great guy but she wasn't there to pick up a great guy. Harper was on the ship to find a wealthy husband.

Her mother was counting on her.

Harper could just imagine Teagan's expression if she told him that she was the sole provider for her mother's nursing care.

The monthly bill was outrageous.

And it seemed each month the amount increased.

All the flowers and sweet words in the world wouldn't pay that bill each month.

And eventually, Teagan would realize he'd bitten off more than he could chew, which would leave her where?

Jaded, bitter and flat-ass broke.

She knew Teagan wouldn't be far behind but maybe if she reached her room in time, she could lock him out and bury herself in bed.

Harper exited the elevator and walked briskly to her room. The second elevator dinged and she sensed, rather than saw, Teagan step out.

Harper turned in spite of herself and swallowed a yelp when she saw his expression.

Teagan looked like he wanted to put her over his knee and spank her raw.

But not in a good way.

"I'm tired," she blurted. Teagan wasn't having it.

"We're having a conversation tonight," he told her firmly, pulling her key card from her fingers and swiping it quickly before pushing the door open. He gestured with a terse "inside," and Harper reluctantly did as she was directed.

Teagan closed the door and locked it. She expected him to light into her immediately but he bypassed her for the bathroom. Harper frowned. Did he barge into her room just to use her toilet? Was that his revenge for rejecting him? Blowing up her bathroom?

But then she heard the water running and she realized he was drawing a bath.

Damn him.

Considerate and sexy.

Knock it off, Carmichael.

"What are you doing?" she asked when he returned, stripping as he went. He dropped his clothes and came for her without answering. Harper squeaked as he pulled the dress up over her head, stopped briefly to kiss her hard, then grabbed her hand and took her to the bathroom.

"Get in," he said, sinking into the tub slowly. He didn't wait for her to acquiesce. It was as if he knew she wouldn't refuse him. That both galled and aroused her.

She wasn't accustomed to taking orders. But there was something a little dangerous about Teagan at the moment that tripped her wires in the biggest way. She stepped into the tub but before she could slide to the opposite end, he curled her into the cove between his legs.

His cock bumped against her behind and she hitched a tight breath as the memory of what he could do with that thing made her blush. "Lean back," he said, the deep rumble of his chest vibrating through the water.

Harper sighed and sank against him, closing her eyes briefly to enjoy the illicit joy of being held against his solid body.

For a long moment, they simply enjoyed the mild jets swirling the water, neither speaking—the air heavy with tension.

"Tell me what you're running from," he said.

"I'm not running from anything."

Teagan tried again, his voice steady but firm. "Tell me what has hurt you so bad that you're unwilling to try again."

Her silence prompted him to start throwing out theories.

"Bad boyfriend broke your heart?"

"I don't allow my heart to be broken," she returned coolly.

"Then tell me why you keep pushing me away when you know we're a good fit in so many ways."

"Teagan, I've tried to spare your feelings," she said, searching for a convincing way to lie. "I'm just not interested in anything serious with you." She turned to face him, meeting his gaze. "If you were interested in just sex, I could handle that. Sex with you is phenomenal, but I can't offer you anything else."

"You've already said all these things but I know you're holding back. If you can tell me truthfully why you won't be with me, I'll leave you alone if that's what you want."

She frowned, not quite believing him. "You're serious?"

"I'm totally serious."

"Can we still have sex?" she asked coyly, warming to his proposal.

"That'll be up to me to decide. Unlike you, I'm all in. I want you, Harper. Whatever it is that you are... I want it. But if I can't have all of you then I'm not sure I want the consolation prize."

Sex with her was the consolation prize? "That's not what most guys say."

"I'm not most guys."

He was right about that. She reached beneath the water and grasped his semiflaccid shaft, giving it a squeeze. "Try to tell me you don't want to bend me over this bathtub and screw me right here."

His gaze darkened with immediate desire and he surged against her hand but he didn't cave. "Tell me and I'll decide from there."

Maybe this was a deal she should take.

Teagan seemed a reasonably sensible guy. Maybe he'd understand the economics she was faced with and agree her options were slim.

Ha. Yeah right.

She could already see the hunger in his eyes, could feel the tension in his frame.

"You talk, I'll wash." Teagan lathered up a soft cloth with body wash and began to lazily rub it across her shoulders and down her back, then back to her front. She smiled in spite of herself when he paused a little too long on her breasts but his touch was incredibly soothing.

"I can't afford to be with you, Teagan," she said, sighing as he sluiced water over her soapy body. It felt wonderful to be pampered by someone who looked at her like Teagan did. Something deeper than lust caressed her senses with that gaze. "My mother has MS and I am her sole caretaker."

He paused with a surprised expression. "That's very noble of you."

"Not noble at all. I'm her only family. She and I are all we have."

"And you thought I would have a problem with you being a good daughter?" he asked quizzically.

If only it were that simple.

She drew a deep breath and took the cloth from his hand to return the favor. "My mother was a hopeless romantic. Always wanting to fall in love. And she fell in love more times than I can count during my childhood. But she was still responsible and made sure my needs were met and we had a roof over our heads. She even managed a small savings. Until Rex came along."

He waited for her to continue. Harper hadn't realized sharing this story would be more difficult than she'd thought.

"Umm, so Rex came into our lives and played the gentleman. He wooed my mom and sold her a million lies just so he could get his hands on her money. By the time my mom figured out she'd been conned, Rex was long gone and so was our entire life savings."

"How much?"

She shrugged, admitting, "It wasn't a lot but it seemed like it to us. Twenty thousand."

"Did your mom file charges?"

She shook her head with a derisive chuckle. "My mom was too embarrassed to admit she'd been played. And she was brokenhearted. She really loved him. Even if it was just an act for Rex." She drew a deep breath as she slid the cloth over his pecs. "My mom got sick not long after. Doctor said stress might've been the catalyst but who knows? Maybe she always would've gotten sick but at least we would've had some money to pay for the doctors."

"Twenty thousand doesn't go far in health care," he said, frowning. "And this guy just disappeared into the wind?"

"Long gone. Sometimes I think about trying to find him but I don't know what I would do if I did. I'm not sure I trust myself. I might just shoot him."

"Do you own a gun?"

"Of course I do."

"Then, you should probably listen to your gut and leave him to his own karma. Even as beautiful as you are, prison orange would not look good on you."

She rinsed the soap away and gently wiped his face, avoiding his eyes. "The thing is, I should perhaps thank him."

"Come again?"

"He taught me that trusting love is for idiots. Love isn't real, Teagan. It's science. A chemical reaction exploding in the brain for a few brief months before reality sets in and the hormone bath subsides."

"Love isn't just about science," he said, pausing to rinse his face. He pushed his hair back and met her gaze. "Love is something you feel here." He tapped her chest where her heart resided. Then, he tapped her forehead. "Not here."

Harper laughed. "Well, maybe for some people, but not me. That's why I'm not the girl for you. I don't believe in love. I believe in hot sex, deep kisses and the power of the dollar. And that's it."

"So you con these men just like that man conned your mother, only your targets are bigger and wealthier," he said, putting together the pieces.

She refused to feel any shame, not in front of Teagan, so she nodded as if proud. "Yep. And I'm good at it. At least I was until you came along."

"You were hurt. That man was an asshole. But you're better than he was," he said, grasping her hands in his.

Harper scowled, irritated that he was trying to save her, as if she needed saving at all. She tugged her hands free. "I like what I do. I like wearing designer clothes and eating at the finest restaurants. I enjoy the privilege of having whatever I want at the snap of a finger. These men fall all over themselves to shower me with gifts and trinkets. And then, when I'm tired of them or our time has run its course… I move on."

"Why Stuart, then?" he asked, peering at her intently, as if knowing Harper had a different agenda than usual. "He's a nice man. And you're not his type."

"I'm all men's type," she disagreed. "If Vanessa hadn't cock-blocked me, I'd have that man in my bed as we speak."

That part was iffy but she wasn't going to admit her failures. She already knew Stuart had been a bad investment of her time, which was simply inexcusable on her part. Now she had to research someone else and so far, she didn't like her options.

A tiny twitch in Teagan's eye gave away his discomfort at her bald statement. She dared him to judge her. "Go ahead, call me a whore, call me a gold digger, it doesn't matter to me. What matters is what lands in my bank account."

"You said you did this for your mother…how much does her care cost?" he asked, throwing her off.

"Why?"

"Because if you're doing this for your mother's care, that other stuff shouldn't matter. The cars, the clothes, the privilege…and honestly, I don't think it does matter to you. I think you're still playing a part and we agreed to complete honesty."

She held her breath as he rose, the water dripping from his magnificent body. He grabbed a towel and wrapped it around his torso as he stepped out.

"The thing is, Harper, you're punishing every man for something that happened to your mother. I understand, but at a certain point, you have to realize that you're wrong."

"Thank you for sharing your unsolicited opinion on my life," she said, grabbing her own towel and tucking it around her. Stepping out, Harper stalked past him, hurt and irritated that he so easily saw around her carefully constructed reasoning.

"And you're wrong," she added. "I do like that stuff. Just because you want to see me in a different light doesn't mean what you want is any more true than what I'm telling you."

"You know how I know you're lying?" he said, stalking closer, crowding her space. "Because of the way your eyes track my every move, how your skin warms to my touch and how your body reacts to mine when you have no choice but to give in. Your mouth can lie but your body does not."

"Sexual attraction isn't an accurate measure of someone's honesty," she said, swallowing the lump in her throat. Everything he said was true but she was also being truthful to a point. "I've never said I didn't respond to your touch. Sex with you is the best I've ever had. You might always have that distinction but I need more than epic sex!"

"Exactly," he said, unswayed by her impassioned response. If she was stubborn, Teagan was equally so. "If we never had sex again, I'd still want to spend every moment with you. You're a hot woman, no doubt, but I'm interested in more than just what's between your legs, sweetheart. Can you say the same about the other men you screw?"

No, she wanted to cry. She was nothing to those other men but they were nothing to her, either, so it was fair, right?

"Teagan," she whispered, losing the will to fight anymore. "I gave you my answer. Either you believe me or you don't."

His jaw firmed and he swept her into his arms, saying in a hard tone, "I don't," before carrying Harper to the bed.

This night would end with both tangled up in each other but Harper knew by morning, everything would look the same.

No matter what Teagan had to say.

20

HE'D MADE HARPER a deal, what more could he say that would convince her to trust him with the truth?

Nothing.

There was nothing left to say or do.

But he couldn't leave without touching her.

No, it wasn't about the sex, but if she wouldn't offer her heart, he'd take what he could get.

He tumbled her to the bed and ripped her towel from her body. Her skin, rosy from the bath, tan from the sun, beckoned to his lips as he bent to press kisses along her tan lines.

Harper shivered, moaning as he slowly opened her legs, splaying those lovely stems so he could feast on the dewy center he craved so much.

Her pale folds, damp and plump, hid that sweet button that he wanted to suck into his mouth.

Harper's scent drove him wild, urged him to bury his face between her thighs and suck and lick until she screamed his name.

Teagan lifted her hips and pulled her close, sinking his tongue deep, sliding and tasting, exploring. He listened for her subtle cues—a tiny gasp, a tight breath, a soft, helpless mewl—and adjusted his tempo, rhythm and pressure until he had her panting like a wild thing in his arms.

The thrill of pleasuring Harper was quickly becoming his favorite activity. She tasted like honey and lemon, pineapple and summer. He would gladly spend the rest of his days camped out, sucking on her swollen nub, listening to the music of her cries.

Teagan had always been a fan of a woman's pussy, but his enjoyment of Harper took that appreciation to a new level.

Was this love?

Was it possible to fall as quickly as that?

Maybe Harper was right and this was just infatuation, or crazy-ass lust that would fade.

His gut called bullshit. This felt right on so many levels.

Why wouldn't she admit the same?

Harper sucked in a tight breath and cried out as she came hard. He tasted her juices, felt her clit pulse with each contraction while her thighs quaked.

Groaning, she allowed him to roll her over to her belly. Her ass was near perfect. She had the trimmest waist that flared to gorgeous, womanly hips. She had a small mole on her right cheek that dared to blemish that soft skin.

His cock surged with need, hard as a manzanita branch. He guided his length to her entrance and slowly pushed inside, breaching her hot sheath. His eyes fluttered shut at the exquisite pleasure, savoring the close heat surrounding his shaft as he buried himself as far as he could possibly go.

"Harper," he breathed in pleasurable agony. "God, girl…"

Still buried inside her, he lifted her onto her knees, pushing her head down to rest on the bedding. She was a carnal offering that he gladly accepted. The twin halves of her ass were perfect for his grip as he thrust against her.

She moaned and curled her fingers into the bedding. The sound of their breathing and their bodies filled the room.

Teagan increased his tempo, losing himself in the intense heat between them. He rocked against her and she pushed to meet him, impaling herself on his shaft, groaning with each thrust.

He gripped her hips harder as the telltale signs of his release began to build. Harper's breathing rasped as she stiffened, keening as another climax found her. Teagan gratefully gave in to the urge to follow.

His thrusts slowed and he finally stopped, withdrawing to fall beside her on the bed, his hand flopping over his eyes.

Neither spoke.

The harsh breathing between them was a shared sound, each heartbeat racing.

"You should go," Harper said, breaking the silence.

He collected her roughly and pulled her against him. "No."

"You promised."

"Go to sleep."

Teagan heard the sadness in her voice, the obvious reluctance to push him out, so he took the burden from her shoulders by refusing.

She seemed relieved and cuddled up to him, falling asleep within moments.

How could someone fight so hard against something they really wanted?

Teagan saw through her motions, recognized the scent of fear in every decision to push him away.

He couldn't force her to trust him.

Either she would come to that realization on her own or she wouldn't.

Teagan had to get to the point where he could watch her walk away if it came to that.

HARPER WAS DREAMING.

She was eleven again in body but her mind was processing the scene as an adult.

The weak sunlight dusted the scarred kitchen table and dust motes danced.

Her mother's tears splashed on the table as she stared at her bank statement.

"He took it all."

The whispered words echoed in the small apartment.

Harper knew how this dream ended because it'd played out in real life.

The scene switched and her mom was on the floor, the strength in her legs giving out.

The scene switched three to four more times, each one filled with more evidence from her past that trusting a man was a lesson in foolishness.

Harper awoke, sweating, around midnight. Teagan was lightly snoring, his deep breathing more soothing than she wanted to admit.

She rolled onto her side and watched Teagan sleep.

Such a classically handsome profile.

If she were a different person, living a different life… yeah, Teagan would've been her first choice.

Funny, kind, sexy—what's not to like?

But surely, that's what her mother must've thought, too, when she met Rex.

Rex had pulled out all the stops to bag her mother.

He'd been a small-time crook but what he'd taken from them might as well have been a million dollars, for it was all they'd had.

At least she could say, the men she took from had plenty to spare.

Justifications, she thought with a derisive smile, *is that what I've come to?*

The thing was, the perfect life was an illusion.

Everyone used everyone else to some varying degree.

So why did she physically hurt at the thought of walking away from Teagan?

It felt perfectly natural to have Teagan in her bed, beside her, laughing with him.

Even arguing.

Harper had always managed to keep a part of herself distant from the men she dated but not with Teagan. It was as if he could psychically rip apart her walls and drag her straight to him.

It was scary and wonderful at the same time.

In the morning, she'd have to find the strength to stick to her guns. Teagan deserved better than she could give him.

Not that she was trying to paint herself as a martyr, but Teagan was a good man and she would ruin him.

In such a short amount of time, Teagan had managed to get under her skin and she hadn't seen it coming.

Teagan stirred, prompting a warm smile on her part. He was so damn cute.

She slid her hand across his belly, intent to rest her head on his shoulder but her hand brushed against a rock-hard erection.

Teagan was fast asleep but his cock was ready to play.

If tonight was all they had left, Harper was going to enjoy every stolen moment.

Burrowing under the light covers, she slipped her mouth over the soft head of his cock, teasing the rim with her tongue.

Teagan groaned and his hips flexed, pushing his shaft deeper into her mouth. She accepted his length and cupped his testicles for a firm squeeze. He groaned more loudly and his hand found her hair, wrapping his strong fingers around her scalp as she worked his erection.

His ball sac tightened beneath her palm as he strained against her mouth. With a guttural cry, he came, flooding her throat with warm, salty fluid in jerking spurts.

She sucked him dry, wanting every drop.

Harper rarely allowed men to come in her mouth.

But she wanted this with Teagan. She wanted to know his taste as well as he knew hers.

With a final sweet lap, she curled her tongue around the fleshy head and he gasped sleepily as he awoke. She emerged from the blankets and he kissed her hard, his tongue swirling into her mouth so that he surely must've tasted himself on her lips.

It was as dirty and wildly arousing as when she'd tasted herself on his mouth, and she was ready to go another round.

She whispered in his ear, "I need you now, Teagan," and he rolled onto his back, taking her with him. Lifting her easily, he helped settle her over his cock, rubbing against the semisoft length, encouraging it to plump back to life.

Teagan was a beast. His stamina was unlike any she'd ever encountered, which worked for her.

This was pure, primal attraction at its wildest form and they were helpless to stop what was building between them.

She winced briefly as she stretched to accommodate his length again but as soon as she sank onto his cock, the tiny annoyance faded and she was left with soul-shivering pleasure.

He held her hips and thrust up into her, jarring her with delicious force.

She groaned his name, rolling her head back, her breasts jutting forward as she rocked on his shaft, working her own magic. His cock rubbed against her G-spot perfectly, the girth of his shaft making it a tight fit inside her.

Teagan slipped his finger between her slippery folds and gently teased her clit. The fluttering touches became maddeningly intense but her orgasm kept skittering out of reach.

Harper growled and pushed back, edging herself a little farther down so that his cock pressed harder against her. *Ohh, that's the spot*, her mouth fell slack as she shuddered with pleasure. "T-Teagan," she gasped, coming hard in giant waves. Her core clenched like a fist, her internal muscles clamping down on his cock, squeezing out his orgasm as he cried out her name.

They climaxed together, their desperate breaths matching each other's as Harper fell forward against his chest, his cock still buried in her pulsing sheath.

"Why are you so good?" she mumbled, still buffeted by

pleasure as her release receded. "Damn you, Teagan. You're a hard habit to quit."

He pressed a kiss to her damp crown and they fell asleep like babies after a long car ride.

Her last thought...

The morning would come too soon.

21

MORNING BROKE AND Harper was still sacked out.

They were sticky with dried sweat and other things.

A shower was in order.

While Teagan waited for Harper to wake, he ordered breakfast for the room, and started the shower.

No time for a bath today.

They were nearing their last port on the cruise and Teagan still hadn't done any souvenir shopping. He wanted to get J.T. something offensive and rude as a thank-you for sending him on this trip.

J.T. would love it; Hope, not so much.

A soft knock at the door alerted him to the room service delivery. He ushered in the man with the breakfast cart, tipped him and then sent him on his way.

Harper, smelling the bacon, opened her eyes blearily to stare uncomprehendingly at the tidy breakfast spread he'd put together.

She rubbed at her eyes and struggled to sit up, holding the sheet to her breasts. "What's going on?" she asked, her voice cracking with residual sleep. "Are those…pancakes?"

"Yeah, I wasn't sure what you liked but judging by your facial expression whenever you ate them, I didn't order poached eggs."

Harper smiled as if amused that he'd noticed and kicked her feet over the side of the bed, wrapping herself in the sheet. She cocked her head to listen. "Is the shower running?"

"Yes. Shower, then breakfast. I didn't expect them to deliver it so soon," he admitted a bit sheepishly. "But I thought we could use a little wash after last night."

Her cheeks flushed but she nodded. She rose on unsteady feet, wincing a little, and he immediately worried he'd hurt her.

"Are you okay?" he asked.

"I'm fine. Just a little sore."

While part of him was concerned for her, he also found Harper incredibly sexy for being able to handle him with minor consequences.

More evidence that they were meant for one another.

He heard the shower door opening and closing.

If she thought she was showering alone, she was wrong.

Teagan joined her, ignoring her small frown and grabbing the soap to lather over her body.

"What are you doing?" she asked. "You don't take no for an answer do you?"

He chuckled. "Turn," he instructed, and she grudgingly complied. He took his time rubbing the soap over her body and between her legs, cleaning her thoroughly. "How bad is your mom's MS?" he asked.

"Pretty bad," she answered, closing her eyes as Teagan rinsed her free of soap. "She's bed-bound at this point. Doctors aren't optimistic."

"I'm sorry to hear that," he said. "There's no treatment or alternative therapy available?"

"They've done it all. It's just not working."

Teagan nodded. "It sucks when there's nothing more you can do to help a loved one," he said. "Does your mother know what you do for a living?"

Harper's frown returned and she gave him her back with

a shrug. "We've never talked about it. Honestly, she has bigger issues, if you know what I mean, than worrying about how I make a dollar."

"You might be surprised."

She huffed an impatient breath and returned to face him. "Just stop it. You don't need to play morality police or whatever role you think you're stepping into. I don't want or need your opinion on how I live my life."

If spikes could've erupted from her skin and skewered him to the glass, he'd be dead.

Talk about a touchy subject.

But in his experience, people who lashed out or reacted poorly to a simple question were usually suffering their own guilt about the situation.

He also knew it wasn't going to end well if he kept poking that sore spot.

"Sorry," he said, lifting his hands in mock surrender. "I overstepped."

"Yeah, you did."

They finished up in silence and stepped out of the shower, wrapping themselves in big, fluffy robes but the tension in the room was palpable.

He knew Harper was about to throw him out so he wasn't surprised when she did exactly that.

She gestured to the breakfast spread and the shower. "This was very nice but I'm going to have to ask you to go. This isn't fun anymore. You're making this situation unbearable and I'm over it. So if you could please just go to your own room, that would be great."

Teagan chuckled with a shake of his head. There was no arguing with her right now. Harper was visibly agitated and he could sense tears weren't far behind, even if her tone was clipped.

"Sure," he said, dropping the robe and walking nude to scoop up his discarded clothes. He was trying to be understanding but his limits were being tested. Why was he chasing a woman who was determined to push him away? If he saw someone else doing what he was doing, he'd call them out as a special kind of stupid. But Harper did weird things to his ability to be rational. "Let me know when you want to pull your head out of your ass."

"Just because I don't want to be with you doesn't mean—"

"Except you do want me. Dammit, Harper, do you think I'm an idiot? You want me as bad as I want you, but there's something in your head that keeps telling you to run."

She tried laughing but the sound was strained. "You don't know me well enough to pass that kind of judgment."

"It's not judgment, it's plain fact. I get it, you were hurt. Bad things happened. But shit, bad things happen to everyone. Are you going to punish everyone around you in the hopes of gaining some kind of satisfaction?"

Harper's stony silence egged him on.

"Yeah, so run. Run like a little girl caught up in an adult's game. Someday you're going to wake up and realize you ran away from all the wrong things. Money sure as hell isn't going to do much for the mountain-sized pile of regret waiting for you if you keep this up."

"Sage advice," she said, sounding bored. "Thank you, Obi-Wan Kenobi. Would you like to share any more clichéd bits of advice before you go?"

"Just this." He jerked Harper to him and kissed her hard. The tiniest moan escaped her lips as he pushed her away. "Looks fade, honey, and then you're left with what you have inside. And right now…you've got a whole lot of nothing. Good luck with that."

Teagan slammed out of Harper's room and bypassed his own, going straight to the workout facility. He needed to burn off some of this anger before he punched a wall.

He didn't know which of them was more stupid—him for wanting her so bad he was willing to make a fool out of himself, or her, for denying herself the one thing that she wanted so badly.

Hell…they were both idiots.

Once Teagan was gone, Harper allowed the tears.

How dare he judge her without knowing the ins and outs of her life?

He didn't know how it felt to watch his mother slowly lose all function, to basically become a human vegetable, kept alive by machines.

She was a survivor, dammit.

Not a victim, not a crybaby.

She'd been given a basket of lemons and she'd damn well made lemon margaritas out of them.

Did he think he could dazzle her with bullshit—all the romancy stuff like breakfast in bed, epic sex, fun times and laughter—when in fact, she knew those were the things that were an illusion?

Men were skilled at wooing a woman when they wanted to catch them.

But keeping up that level of intense courtship…impossible.

Which was why Harper was happy to move on when that happened.

No hard feelings. Just a fatter bank account.

Sure, there were nights when she wanted to cry herself to sleep.

Of course, there were days when she wanted to vomit at the knowledge she had to have sex with her "boyfriend," but those inconvenient moments faded fast enough when she made her deposits.

Stuart was going to be the different one.

She wanted a nice man with a fat bank account who would treat her well enough that she could retire.

But Stuart wanted Vanessa.

So now she was looking at moving on to her next target and she wanted to scream.

Harper didn't want any of them.

Harper wanted a man with big, strong shoulders, an easy smile, to-die-for eyes and a cock that would split most women in two.

Her shoulders shook as she buried her face in her hands.

She wanted Teagan.

She wanted him so bad.

Her chest felt as if it were caving in, the words in her mouth had tasted wooden.

How could she tell him he was right but even so, nothing changed?

This was the hand she'd been dealt.

Teagan Carmichael wasn't meant to be hers.

Some woman was going to be the luckiest in the world but Harper wasn't the one.

A spurt of illogical jealousy burned in her chest at this fictitious woman who would someday have Teagan's heart.

Teagan...

Why?

Hadn't she been through enough that fate could've been a little nicer?

Maybe if Teagan had been a sloppy kisser or a total buffoon between the sheets, she could've easily dismissed the attraction between them.

But that's not what'd happened. Teagan pushed all the right buttons.

And even some buttons she hadn't known existed.

If Teagan had been rich that would've solved everything.

But Teagan was a regular guy.

Hardworking, honest, kind, sexy...but not wealthy.

He couldn't help her with her mom.

He couldn't pad her bank account.

He wouldn't buy her fancy jewels or expensive trips.

But he'd sure as hell love her from the tips of her toes to the top of her head.

Why couldn't that be enough?

Harper dried her tears and wiped her nose on the sleeve of her robe. Life wasn't fair, she reminded herself dully as she plucked a strawberry from a bowl. Sometimes life was seriously messed up.

She flopped back on the bed and Teagan's scent enveloped her. Harper rolled onto her side, burying her nose in the bedding, inhaling every last molecule she could. He even smelled like heaven.

Right about now, she wished she had more female friends. But friends, much less other women, were not only a luxury but a liability.

Case in point, Vanessa was awesome.

Kinda like a mom, but the cool mom everyone wants to be around. But not so cool that she lets her kid be stupid and ruin their life.

And she hoped to compete with that?

Vanessa had genuine sexiness down to a science.

And Harper couldn't bring herself to hate her because Vanessa was amazing.

Failure tasted bitter, but no more so than the realization that she was losing her ability to snap a finger and get what she wanted from men.

The crazy part was, while it might sting her ego, in the back of her mind she was a little relieved, too.

Harper was plain tired of the game. The constant strategy, the manipulation and lies.

Being with Teagan had reminded her what real happiness could feel like.

Not the shallow, brief flash of pleasure that came with new trinkets or gifts.

Keep talking yourself in a corner, that's productive.

The derision in her own thoughts was a slap in the face,

a good reminder that pity parties were unproductive and useless.

If she wanted the freedom to live her own life, she had to accept that ambition came with a cost.

Rising from the bed, she jerked the bedsheets off and tossed them in a pile to the floor. She wanted fresh sheets tonight. There was no way she was going to fall asleep with any peace if she had Teagan in her nose all night.

Bypassing the wonderful spread Teagan had ordered, she went to the bathroom to prepare for her day.

One foot in front of the other, that's how it's done.

No more whining about what could've been.

No more melancholy over what she'll never have.

Hearts mend. Memories fade.

She just needed a little time and distance to realize that Teagan had only been a fun diversion.

In the meantime, it was a big ship—she'd just avoid him.

22

TEAGAN RESISTED THE urge to pound on Harper's door. In fact, when his feet wanted him to take a detour toward Harper's room, he deliberately went the opposite direction, even taking the longer route to the elevator, just to avoid temptation.

Every man had his limits.

There were only so many times he could bounce back from rejection.

He wanted to shake off the bitter, sour mood he seemed stuck in but every time he replayed the scene in his head with Harper, the anger ballooned.

Selfish little shit.

Was it uncharitable of him to think that way about Harper?

Maybe.

She had her reasons.

But it didn't stop him from wanting to shake her head off her shoulders.

A rough chuckle escaped him as he returned to the gym for another punishing workout.

Burning off the rage and frustration seemed the only way to get through the chaos messing with his brain.

He'd never been so wrapped up in a woman before.

Honestly, the situation with Harper felt like it was happening to someone else.

He was the easygoing one; the Carmichael with a live-and-let-live attitude toward life.

Until Harper.

Climbing onto the treadmill, he did a quick warm-up, then set a brisk pace. He wanted to run so hard that his muscles screamed for every bit of his attention. He didn't want the ability to think about Harper for a second.

Pushing hard, he did exactly that until he was panting, sweat pouring down his face, and exhausted.

Cycling down, he toweled off, cooled down and grabbed his workout bag to shower when he nearly ran into Harper as she came in.

The awkward tension between them was hard to ignore.

Immediately, he wanted to kiss her.

Angry kisses for sure, but putting his lips on hers seemed like the best idea ever.

By the grace of God, he found the strength to resist.

When Harper opened her mouth to say something, he sidestepped her and kept walking.

He wasn't going to play games anymore.

Harper had said her piece and he was going to respect her fool-ass decision.

He'd just have to find a way to deal with the disappointment.

And the yawning hole cracking open in his chest where his heart used to be.

Teagan spent the day at their last port looking for chintzy souvenirs to bring back to his friends and brother.

They'd all appreciate the boy humor of fart shirts, dancing naked ladies on a pen and scorpion candies.

For Hope, he went with something a bit classier—a hand-crafted artisan necklace by a local artist.

But even as he enjoyed doing a little shopping, seeing

the sights and just being a tourist, in the back of his mind, Harper remained.

What was she doing?

Was she shopping for trinkets, too?

And he couldn't quite help admiring a dress that he thought would look spectacular on her.

He was seconds away from throwing down some cash when he came to his senses and walked away.

He'd already bought her a dress she refused to wear, why spend more on a lost cause?

Plenty of fish in the sea, as his brother would say.

But he imagined what J.T. would've said if Teagan had offered that same clichéd statement in regards to Hope, if things hadn't worked out the way they had.

A middle finger might've been involved.

Teagan felt that way right now.

A giant middle finger to everyone.

Including Harper.

As he was finishing up, he saw Vanessa and Stuart shopping together. Their laughter rang through the stalls as they held hands, beamed at each other and looked like newlyweds.

They looked good together and he was happy for them.

And he meant that without any snark or self-pity.

It was amazing how quickly you could bond with a total stranger.

Vanessa saw him first and immediately waved him over. He planned to decline but he knew that Vanessa wouldn't take no for an answer.

Seeing as it was their last night in port, he figured it wouldn't hurt to say goodbye.

"You look like you're doing your part to shore up Mexico's economy," he joked, gesturing to Vanessa's bag filled with odds and ends.

"Oh, honey, this is nothing. I have things being shipped, too," Vanessa said with a wink.

Stuart chuckled. "The lady loves her cultural art."

"Art is what separates us from the beasts," Vanessa reminded him with a cheeky grin.

They were almost too sweet for words. He hoped it worked out for them in the long run.

"What kind of goodies do you have?" Vanessa asked, wanting a peek.

"Just your classic guy stuff. Bathroom humor."

Stuart grinned. "Classic. Always good for a laugh."

He nodded. "Right?"

Stuart realized Teagan was alone and a subtle frown creased his brow. "Where's your young lady?"

"She isn't interested in being my lady, unfortunately," he answered, going for honesty. It would've been easier to lie but he liked Stuart and he didn't see a reason to hide the truth. "I tried, but she's looking for something different than what I can offer."

Stuart's understanding warred with Vanessa's expression of determination.

"You have a look that's kinda scaring me," he said to Vanessa. "She's made her choice and I respect it. My dignity can't take another hit by chasing after a woman who doesn't want me."

"Oh, the girl has her head up her ass. She wants you. It's plain to everyone but her."

"Be that as it may, Teagan is right to respect her decision," Stuart added with a meaningful look to Vanessa.

But Vanessa rolled her eyes. "Forgive me, my handsome bald hero, but girls like Harper who think they know everything are about as clueless as a newborn when it comes to the stuff that really matters."

"Harper's pretty clear in what she wants."

"Poppycock."

Teagan chuckled, amused that Vanessa was so fired up on his behalf, but he figured it was time to let them finish their shopping without his interference. "It's been a pleasure to get to know you both. I hope we can stay in touch," he said, by way of courtesy. Not that he didn't mean it, but he knew realistically, chances were slim that they'd ever see one another again.

But Stuart surprised him when he produced a business card and flipped it to scribble his personal cell number on the back. "Good men are hard to find in this world. If you're interested, let's talk about working together."

Flabbergasted, he stared at Stuart. "Not that I'm not flattered as hell, but what could I possibly do for you?"

"You're a pilot. A highly decorated airman. And you've got a solid head on your shoulders. That's exactly the kind of man I like to have working for me and I just happen to need a private pilot. Let me know if you're interested."

Teagan stared at the opportunity in his hand, unable to believe a billionaire like Stuart Buck was willing to hire a man he'd met days ago.

"I'm…hell, I'm speechless," he admitted.

Vanessa laughed and said, "Well, keep your schedule clear because we fully expect you to be at our wedding, too."

"Wedding?" he repeated, shocked. "You two? Already talking about marriage?"

Stuart placed a hand on his shoulder. "Son, when you've lived a life like mine, you realize that when good things come to you, you grab on with both hands. I listen to my gut and it never steers me wrong. My gut says Vanessa is the girl for me. I never thought I'd meet another woman I could love as much as my first wife. Fate proved me wrong. Time doesn't matter when you feel in your bones what's right."

"I'm stunned but super happy for you," he finally said, breaking into a big grin. "Holy hell, I'm jealous, too. But mostly really stoked for you two. That's fantastic."

Vanessa smiled sweetly and pressed a motherly kiss on his cheek, a far cry from the first time she'd laid eyes on Teagan, and said, "Don't give up on that fool girl. You're what she needs. Even if she's too blind to see it."

Stuart slapped Teagan on the back and said, "Look forward to hearing from you," and they went about their shopping, their hands locking together as if fused.

Damn. Isn't that a turn of events?

If only he and Harper had been so lucky.

Teagan stared at the business card in his hand and realized this would change everything.

He'd wanted out of the charter business even before sales had stagnated, but his loyalty to J.T. had kept him plugging on.

Then, when the business had been destroyed and effectively rebuilt from the ground up, he'd let J.T. take the reins in the hopes that J.T. would want to explore taking over Blue Yonder for good.

Now that path seemed to be materializing before his eyes and he couldn't quite shake the feeling that he was dreaming.

Except, he wanted to share this news with Harper and that wasn't going to happen.

Still, good news needed to be celebrated.

Which meant, he needed to turn his cell back on and call his brother.

Knowing J.T., he'd probably left a million messages just to see what he was up to.

Well, wait until Teagan shared what was going on.

He couldn't believe it.

But he'd take it.

And if his excitement was slightly dimmed because he didn't have Harper to share it with, he'd just have to accept the facts as they were and move on.

Opportunity didn't wait for lovesick hearts to mend.

THE REST OF the cruise passed quickly as they churned through the water to return to Los Angeles. Aside from that one unfortunate brush with Teagan at the gym, she'd managed to avoid seeing him, which was a blessing.

Resisting the need to see him, to feel him pressed against her, had become an almost physical ailment that she suffered through only by focusing on her next target.

The research phase was the most time-consuming, so she used her downtime to bury herself in notes and strategy.

At the very least, this phase kept her attention riveted to the task. She felt nothing as she assembled pictures, articles, did background research and pulled financials.

She was detached from the process as she efficiently complied a neat portfolio of her next target, choosing to bypass her previous alternates in favor of an Italian businessman.

Billionaire Vincent Dario had a taste for fine women and wine and was currently searching for his next conquest.

He wasn't kind or compassionate like Stuart—ruthless and self-serving was more his speed—and he was known to be a bit of a pervert behind closed doors.

But he was loaded.

As in, filthy, obscenely loaded, and Harper needed a fat payday if she hoped to retire with even a decent savings account.

No more spending frivolously on designer clothes and shoes. She wanted out of this lifestyle for good.

But she couldn't quit until she had a certain amount squirreled away in her bank.

Which meant, she had to suck it up, stop mooning over Teagan, and get her head in the game.

Vincent wasn't unattractive—dark hair, dark eyes, a slightly paunchy belly, but only marginally so, and a sharp wit.

At least she wouldn't die of boredom.

It was difficult to play the part of the vapid arm candy for too long before she wanted to stab her own eyeballs out.

But even when she knew that was the course of action she needed to take, it didn't mean there weren't times when she closed her eyes and wished for something different.

In her private moments, she replayed Teagan's smile in her memory—the way his eyes lit up when he laughed, how safe and secure she'd felt in his arms—and then, when she felt the sadness tug too strongly, she shut down those thoughts and returned to her task.

By the time they reached LA again, she was ready to move forward, even if she wasn't entirely excited about the job.

However, she was surprised to see Vanessa at her door the morning they were docked.

She pressed a card into Harper's hand. "When you come to your senses, give me a call. In the meantime, keep yourself out of trouble."

Vanessa gave Harper's cheek a pat and went on her way, pulling her travel luggage behind her with that signature sassy walk that only Vanessa could pull off without looking tawdry.

Harper stared down at the business card in her hand and noted it was one of Stuart's. She chuckled at the older woman's panache. On the back was a cell number.

She knew she wouldn't call.

But Harper curled that card in her palm as if it were a treasure.

With a sigh, she tucked the card into her purse and grabbed her luggage, ready to put this trip behind her.

No sense in dwelling.

Harper managed to get off the ship without running into Teagan but her heart was beating furiously at the fear she might.

Then she fought with the irrational disappointment that she hadn't.

Make up your damn mind.

Harper squared her shoulders and called an Uber to pick her up.

This was the strangest trip she'd ever experienced—and one she'd never forget.

23

TEAGAN WALKED INTO Blue Yonder Charter and immediately J.T. folded him into a big, manly hug, before assessing him critically.

"I expected you to be more tan," he said.

"Well, sunscreen is your friend, buddy," Teagan replied, dropping his bag on the floor. "I could use a beer, though."

J.T. tossed him a beer from the minifridge as Teagan dropped into his chair with a sigh. "What a trip, right?"

"You could say that." Teagan took a long guzzle of his beer, burped and met his brother's gaze. "Never buy me a vacation again. Especially not a singles cruise."

"It was Kirk's idea. I wanted to send you to Jamaica for Hedonism but he said that wasn't your speed."

"Well, thank God for small favors," he quipped. "Yeah, not sure a swingers resort would've been my thing."

"Yeah, I guess not. So what happened? You shut your phone off and I couldn't get ahold of you, and then you call me out of the blue with this opportunity to be a pilot for some billionaire you met on the ship? Are you for real?"

"As real as a heart attack. I can't believe it myself. Stuart Buck is legit."

"How'd you manage to find yourself in his radar?" J.T. asked.

"Extreme luck."

J.T. grinned. "And here I thought I was the lucky one." Sobering, he asked, "So, what did you decide?"

"Hell, I don't know. I like running Blue Yonder with you—and a brand-new plane is pretty exciting—but you already know that I was starting to think the charter business wasn't the right fit for me."

J.T. nodded. "I know, bro. I also know you kept going because of me. So, whatever you decide, I'll support you."

"Really?"

"Yeah."

"To be truthful, I kinda expected more of a fight from you," Teagan admitted with a short laugh. "The last time I even breathed a word about leaving Blue Yonder, you threw a huge hissy fit."

"I don't remember it that way," J.T. said, even though they both knew that was the case. But then J.T. added, "Okay, so yeah, I didn't take it very well. But I felt like a failure, you know? I mean, the business was failing and you were itching to bail…it just felt like a huge ton of bricks on my shoulders and I felt bad for dragging you down with me."

"You never dragged me down," Teagan said, setting his brother straight. "Look, we both needed Blue Yonder when we started the business. But things have changed. *You've* changed. You're ready to take the wheel on your own, if that's what you want. I'm just more interested in a steady gig at this point in my life."

"And squiring around a billionaire sounds like a cush job." J.T. gave him a shit-eating grin. "You'd be stupid to pass up this kind of opportunity and I'd kick your ass if you did."

"I'd like to see you try," Teagan drawled, his mouth twitching. "I can still beat you in hand to hand."

"Care to wager?"

But Teagan wasn't sure he'd win that bet. They were both in good shape—military habits died hard—but J.T.

was younger and built beefier. Plus, Teagan didn't want his little brother getting the idea that he could whoop him, so he wasn't going to take the chance. "Look, what I'm saying is...you can have Blue Yonder if you're open to running it on your own. I think I'm going to take Stuart up on his offer."

"Good." J.T. nodded in agreement. "And yes, I'll take Blue Yonder off your hands."

"I'll even give you a good price for my share," Teagan offered and J.T. did a double take. "What? You think I'm just giving the business to you on a silver platter? That's what your girlfriend is for. Pay up, little brother."

"Hell no, you greedy asshole," J.T. said, countering with, "I'll offer you a fair buyout price."

"You expect me to pay you to get out of our business? Sounds like double-dipping to me."

J.T. hooked his arm around Teagan's neck playfully. "Don't worry, we'll hash out the details, but in the meantime, you're going to tell me all about the wild hook-ups you had so I can live vicariously through you."

"Trouble in paradise?" he asked, mildly concerned.

"No, not at all. I'm just a horny bastard," J.T. answered without a hint of shame. "Now, fess up...how hot was that cruise?"

Teagan laughed at J.T.'s insistence to know details, called him a "gossipy girl" but decided to share his experience with Harper, even down to the fact that he still wanted her but she didn't want him.

J.T. grabbed two more beers and tossed one to Teagan. "Serious? That's some messed-up shit. A real live gold digger. I thought that was sort of a cliché. I didn't realize it actually happened to people, but then, I'm not in the right tax bracket for anyone to try it on me."

"I don't want to say she's doing it for a noble reason but I kinda understand her drive. Her mom is real sick and she needs the money to take care of her."

"Sort of noble," J.T. agreed with a confounded expression. "But isn't there another way? I mean, some kind of social program that can help out or something. Obamacare?"

"Hell, I don't know. It doesn't really matter, though. She's handling the situation the way she sees fit and she doesn't see me in her equation. I'm respecting her wishes and backing off."

"You love her." J.T. called it like it was. And yeah, he was right. Teagan shrugged with a nod. "Then, what the hell, you pussy, why are you giving up?"

"C'mon, J.T., I'm not about to chase after a woman when she plainly, in good English, told me to screw off. I do have some dignity to cling to."

"Sometimes women don't know what they want," J.T. said with a sage sigh, as if he were suddenly the guru of the opposite sex. "Sometimes we have to help them figure out what they really want."

"I can only imagine what Hope would have to say about that statement," Teagan returned drily as he tipped back his beer. "And you're an idiot if you believe that anyway."

"No, seriously, I don't mean it in a disrespectful way. I mean it as sometimes women, as the smarter sex, get lost in the details, too tripped up on the whys and hows instead of following their gut and just going for it. Does Hope look like the kind of woman who would give me a chance? Hell no. But we work. She's the yin to my yang."

"I get it," Teagan said, rolling his eyes. "You're very happy together as complete opposites. Get to the real point."

"The real point is, sometimes you have to smash through all the distractions and just fill their scope with nothing but reasons why you work. Only then will they realize that the trees were in the way the whole time so they couldn't see the ocean."

"You make absolutely no sense."

J.T. gestured impatiently. "You know what I mean...that saying..."

"Can't see the forest for the trees?" Teagan offered, wish-

ing J.T. had spent a little more time with his education and a
little less time messing around. "Yeah, I see what you're saying. Maybe. But Harper's unlike any woman I've ever met."

"That's what makes her special. Hope was so far outside
of my wheelhouse. Smart, sexy, funny, a *friggin' scientist*,
you know? But man, that redhead got me by the short hairs
and I couldn't imagine life without her. Is that how you feel
about this Harper?"

His little brother was giving him love advice.

The irony was astounding.

But Teagan had to admit, the kid made some sense.

How did he truly feel about Harper?

He missed the scent of her hair on the pillow, the feel of
her against his body, the way she never passed up an opportunity to keep him on his toes…

And that ache in the center of his chest seemed to grow
with each passing day.

Yeah, maybe he couldn't imagine his life without her.

But the problem remained…this wasn't a one-way street.

Harper had to be willing to travel the same road and she
plainly wasn't.

Teagan smiled, grateful for his brother's support, but he
had to let Harper go. "I appreciate all you've said. I'll give
it some thought," he said, knowing if he didn't throw his
brother a bone, he would worry at it forever. "But for now
I gotta do what's right for me and that's calling Stuart to
accept his offer."

J.T. jerked a nod of understanding before tipping his beer.
"She must've been something else to turn your head like
this. I hope you guys get things figured out."

Teagan rose and deposited his empty beer bottle in the
recycle, murmuring, "Yeah, she was," before heading out
to the hangar to check out the new plane.

HARPER SMILED AT Vincent across from the elegant table,
the ambient sounds of the upscale restaurant irritating her.

The place was so pretentious. She minced her tiny salmon filet with dainty strokes, taking a demure bite as Vincent rambled on about—what the hell *was* he talking about?—and pretended to care.

She looked flawless from her fingertips to her toes. Not a hair out of place.

But she'd rather be anywhere but in that restaurant.

The permanent smile on her face was likely to freeze that way, but things were progressing nicely with Vincent and she didn't want to jeopardize all the progress she'd made.

So far she'd been able to sidestep any sexual intimacy with him, but she knew that grace period was coming to a close. Vincent was going to expect something for his troubles at this point.

Tonight was as good a time as any, she supposed.

But the thought left her cold.

If her vagina could've clamped shut and locked tight with a padlock, it would've.

Vincent had already taken it upon himself to show her his manhood, wagging it around like it was a prize. Thankfully, he'd been too drunk to do anything after his show-and-tell, passing out, naked and snoring on the sofa. Counting her lucky stars, she'd been happy to ditch him without raising suspicion.

However, she could only stall for so long.

She would have to let the "Italian Stallion" have his night.

As if that wasn't enough of a distraction, Harper had visited her mother earlier that morning.

Anna was deteriorating fast. There was really nothing that could be done. The doctors had assured her that her mom was not suffering, that she wasn't in pain.

But it killed Harper to know that it didn't matter how expensive the care or how fine the facility, Anna was never going to get better.

Her mother had lived a sad, desperate life, hoping to find

someone who loved her and had been used and abused by every single man she'd brought home.

Why did some women rise and some women fall when life tried to kick them down?

Maybe if Anna had been more like Vanessa...

Dangerous thinking, she reminded herself. *It is what it is*.

She pressed the luxurious linen to the corners of her mouth and pretended to be full, even though that sliver of filet hadn't been big enough to satisfy a child.

Vincent, on the other hand, was already looking at dessert and leering at her as he said, "I could order something to go and lick it off your beautiful body."

Yes, I'll take the bladder infection to go, thank you.

The words burned on her tongue but she choked them back, answering with a sweet smile, "Darling, you spoil me."

Vincent beamed, pleased. He gestured to the server. "Bring me your finest chocolate mousse to go."

Then he returned to Harper with a spark in his eye. "I've been waiting for this night. I'm going to make love to you like no one ever has before."

Not likely.

Harper pretended to blush but remained silent. She didn't trust herself not to say something acidic or at the very least sarcastic.

The little pickle in Vincent's pants wasn't much to work with but she'd succeeded with worse. Besides, it wasn't her pleasure she was after. As long as Vincent saw stars and would do anything to keep her happy, her vibrator would keep her satisfied.

Along with memories of Teagan.

This time the blush was real. Not a night had gone by that she hadn't pleasured herself to the desperate memory of Teagan's body on hers, the feeling of his cock filling and stretching her, that exquisite pain-pleasure of being impaled on a man like Teagan…*oh, goodness*…it was enough to go from stone-cold to raging inferno in moments.

Vincent mistook her reaction and chuckled. "My little sex kitten is impatient," he said, further pleased. "I like your neediness for my cock."

Blech.

Could she pull this off?

She was starting to feel queasy.

Just ride it through, no big deal. Think of the prize.

But Teagan was in her head.

She missed his smile.

She missed the way he had a particular way of looking at her when he wanted to throw her to the bed and have his way with her.

Hell, she missed the way he called her out on her own bullshit.

Good grief, Vincent was still talking.

"I dream about you, kitten. Deep, wet, hot dreams where I devour your lithesome body inch by inch."

Vincent was trying his hardest to be sexy. And maybe if she weren't in such a bad state of mind, she might've bought it, but as it was she just wanted to scrub her face, throw her hair in a bun and watch Netflix with a bowl of popcorn.

No, a damn *loaded* hamburger dripping with cheese, because her stomach was caving in from that tiny morsel passing itself off as a main entrée.

Instead of responding, she faked a tiny shiver, which seemed to be enough for Vincent.

He called for the check, which arrived along with a pretty box filled with their mousse to go, and Vincent rose to take her hand in his. "Come, kitten. Tonight I will make your dreams come true."

Gag.

Barf.

God, open a hole beneath my feet and swallow me whole.

But seeing as God wasn't answering fervent prayers at

the moment, she had no choice but to allow Vincent to whisk her away to his palatial—and gaudy—mansion for a night she'd rather forget.

The ride was short and soon they were in the house. She'd been here before many times. Vincent enjoyed showing off his wealth. She'd been appropriately wowed, if not privately turned off by all the ridiculous opulence, and after playing to his ego enough, Vincent had rewarded her with a diamond tennis bracelet, which she was wearing tonight.

"I'd love a glass of wine," she said abruptly with a bright smile when he started to lead her upstairs to the bedroom. "Something red, perhaps?"

"Of course, kitten. You have nerves," Vincent allowed with an indulgent smile. "I shall be gentle our first time but you shall have your wine if you wish it. Await me in the sitting room."

"Thank you," she said gratefully, letting out a breath as he disappeared, humming as he went in a deep baritone. She fished in her purse and pulled out a single Benadryl. It wouldn't kill him but it would hopefully knock him out.

Vincent reappeared with two glasses and she accepted hers with a sweet smile. He closed his eyes for a healthy sip and she stealthily opened the capsule to pour into her wineglass.

Then, she swirled the wine with her finger, mixing it up before he reopened his eyes. She approached him with a sultry smile, dragging her wet finger along the rim of her glass. His eyes glazed immediately as she darted her tongue out to lick her lips.

Harper crowded his personal space so that he could feel the softness of her breasts against his chest.

"You know what I want?" she asked in a husky whisper in his ear. He gulped and she said, "I want to taste where your lips have been..."

Then she took his glass and made a big deal out of sipping where his mouth had been. She ran her tongue along the rim as she had her finger, enjoying how easily the older man became a puppy dog in her hands.

"You are sex incarnate," he breathed and she laughed lightly, teasing him more.

"Let me help you," she said, lifting her own glass to his lips. "Drink, Vincent. Open your mouth and take it all in. I want to watch you swallow every drop."

She brought his original glass to her own lips and allowed a tiny sip to slide down her throat.

"Anything you say," he gasped, greedily gulping the wine so he could put his hands on her.

Vincent finished the wine and eagerly reached for Harper but she danced out of his reach. "Not so fast… I want you to work for it."

Her coy request was just dominant enough to throw Vincent off guard, but still kittenish enough that he was willing to do whatever she asked.

It was a delicate balance—one she'd mastered.

"What do you desire?" Vincent asked, licking his lips, desperate, training his gaze on her chest. She could practically feel the lust shaking his body. "Anything, *bella*!"

Gritting her teeth, she allowed her dress to fall to the floor in a slinky puddle, revealing her matching pink-and-black bra and panty set. She made sure to give him an eyeful before turning and saying, "I need a massage."

"I'll call my masseuse right now," he said feverishly but she stopped him with a petulant look.

"I want *your* hands on my body, Vincent, not a stranger's."

His face flushed with pleasure. "Yes, yes," he said as she reclined on the plush leather chaise like a goddess ready to be fed grapes.

She gestured to her prettily painted toes. "Start here," she instructed.

Hopefully, by the time he reached her thighs, he'd be out.

His beefy hands were neither gentle nor intuitive, which

told her he'd likely be a bumbling boar in bed, but that wasn't happening tonight.

Next time, she'd come prepared with a Xanax so she could get through sex without drugging him to get out of it.

She pretended to moan with pleasure as he ground on her feet, privately wincing as he tried to rub a hole in the sole of her foot until she gestured for him to move to her legs.

His gaze widened as he slid his hands up her legs, trying to creep up her thighs to her lady parts but she shook her finger at him with a playful "no, no, naughty boy" and he returned to her legs with a chastised expression.

At least he wasn't digging into her legs as he had her feet. It was almost pleasant but her thoughts were filled with too much regret to enjoy even the smallest pleasure.

Had she run from Teagan because she was afraid of being hurt or had she run because she was afraid of being used?

Either explanation worked.

But she knew in her heart that Teagan would never hurt her.

Or did she?

Surely her mom had felt that way about Rex, too.

Love messed with the brain.

There was no way she could be trusted to know the right path with all those love hormones playing ping-pong with her mind.

Vincent edged closer to her inner thigh and she forced a giggle. *When was that damn Benadryl going to kick in?*

Not soon enough.

But just as she thought she was going to have to let him play with her breasts or something, his eyelids started to drag.

"Vincent…are you okay?" she asked with pretend concern. "Are you feeling all right? You look very pale."

"I am suddenly very tired," he answered, rocking back on his heels and rubbing his forehead. Distress colored his voice as he said, "I will power through for you, my love. I will not disappoint you again."

"You could never disappoint me," she said, smoothing his cheeks with her hands.

He launched at her face, smothering her with a kiss that made her want to vomit.

His tongue darted into her mouth like a heat-seeking missile and she could do nothing but try to accommodate his sloppy attempts.

But he pulled away with a groan, rubbing his eyes. "I am suddenly exhausted."

"Darling, you need to rest, then," she said, jumping off the chaise to help him stand. "Your health is more important to me than my own pleasure. Please…let me help you to bed."

"Yes, my kitten. That is best," he said, weary. "I promise…tomorrow I will make it up to you. I will make love to you until you cannot walk."

Not with that tiny pickle, she wanted to quip but just smiled.

"I will make you climax many times," Vincent continued as they walked upstairs to his bedroom. "I will make you scream my name."

"Of course you will. I look forward to it," she lied, helping him into his bed. He patted the place beside him but she shook her head regretfully. "I would never dream of disturbing your rest. You need uninterrupted sleep and I can't guarantee that I will be able to keep my hands to myself."

He chuckled weakly as if that were a completely plausible reason and nodded. "My driver will take you home, my kitten. You are a good girl. I will deck you out in sapphires and rubies for your sweetness."

Ordinarily, that promise would've thrilled her to pieces but she felt nothing.

She didn't want jewels anymore.

She didn't want anything Vincent could offer.

She wanted Teagan.

But after everything, she was probably the last person Teagan ever wanted to see again.

24

TEAGAN MET STUART at his office in downtown Los Angeles and quietly marveled at how the building matched Stuart's down-to-earth style.

In his limited experience, those with money tended to go for a modern industrial look but Stuart's office was almost cozy, and he said *almost* because nothing as big as his building could actually qualify as anything close to cozy.

But it was comfortable.

Stuart broke into a big smile as Teagan walked in and he immediately rose to greet him as if they were old friends, instead of potential employer and employee.

"How are you?" Stuart asked, gesturing for Teagan to take a seat opposite him on the sofa set instead of across the desk. "It's been weeks since the cruise. I was very happy to receive your call. I was a little afraid my offer wasn't quite exciting enough for someone like you."

"Exciting enough?" Teagan repeated with a quizzical smile, prompting Stuart to explain.

"Well, with your history in the military and then that daring rescue from Mexican nationals to save your brother, I figured you might need something a little more thrilling than squiring my old behind around."

"Nothing could be further from the truth," he admitted.

"I'm ready for stability. I'm ready to build something that I can retire with. My military pension isn't bad but I'd like to have a little more breathing room."

"Of course, of course," Stuart agreed. "So, I already know your qualifications and I like you a helluva lot so all that remains is to ask, are you interested?"

Teagan didn't know how to delicately ask what the salary would be but Stuart had already thought of everything. He pulled a folded piece of paper from his interior jacket and slid it over to Teagan.

"What's this?"

"Your starting salary."

Teagan stared at the number.

So many zeroes.

His gaze flew to Stuart. "That's too much," he managed to say, though his lips suddenly felt numb. "Hell, that's… that's just kind of ridiculous money to offer me."

"I pride myself on knowing when I see talent. I see it in you. And I'll be truthful, I have friends in high places, I've read more than what most people can see from your military history. You're an amazing pilot. I would consider it an honor to call you a friend and my personal pilot."

"You're serious?"

"As a heart attack, although Vanessa says I need to stop saying that because it's tempting fate."

He smiled at the mention of Vanessa. "You're still going strong?" Teagan asked.

"She's the moon to my stars."

Teagan cracked a smile at the older man's poetic statement. "That's great."

"How about you and that little firecracker, Harper?"

His smile faded but he tried to put a good face on it. "Wasn't in the cards for us, unfortunately. We went our separate ways after the cruise."

"That's a shame," Stuart said, nodding. "She seemed real taken with you."

Teagan didn't want to talk about Harper. Too many nights spent replaying memories that both scalded and made him yearn for more had plagued him since the cruise. Gently redirecting the conversation, he said, "I accept your offer. When do I start?"

Stuart slapped his own knee with enthusiasm. "Excellent! That's exactly what I'd hoped you'd say. I took the liberty of starting your paperwork with my secretary. All I need is your John Hancock on a few papers and we're good to start talking schedules."

They talked shop for the next half hour, then Teagan signed his life away for a boatload of money.

Teagan was still a bit dazed at the number of zeroes in Stuart's offer. He never imagined making that kind of money in his lifetime, much less a year.

But hell, Teagan wasn't opposed to trying it out.

As he was leaving, Stuart handed him a gilded invitation.

"For the wedding," he explained.

Teagan grinned, happy for them. "Wouldn't miss it."

"You better not, you're my best man."

Teagan stared, stunned. "Come again?"

Stuart laughed at Teagan's surprise. "I know, I know, you're probably thinking why would I ask you to fill that role when we hardly know each other but, like I said, I have a feeling about you. So, say yes and I'll have my tailor fix you up with an appropriate monkey suit."

Things were moving at the speed of light.

Teagan could only nod in shock. Stuart pumped his hand in a solid handshake, man to man.

"I'll see you in a week, my boy," Stuart said. "After the wedding, we'll talk in more depth about your responsibilities. I'll be in touch."

Teagan was left to puzzle over what'd all just happened. It felt dreamlike.

The job, the wedding, the sudden change in his lifestyle that was going to throw his world upside down…

All of it.

And the one person he wanted to share all the craziness with was the one person who didn't want him.

Thankfully, he had a feeling Stuart was going to keep him so busy, he wouldn't have any more time to miss Harper.

And he was ready for that blessed relief.

HARPER ANSWERED HER front door and found a courier standing with a huge dress box and a gilded invitation in his hand. "Miss Harper Riley?" he confirmed. At her confused nod, he had her sign for the package and then handed off the box and letter with a short bow as he left.

Surely this had to be from Vincent, right?

But Vincent's gift-giving style was more in keeping with Tiffany's than Vera Wang.

Harper carefully untied the ornate box to reveal an exquisite dress nestled in delicate tissue paper.

"Goodness gracious me," she breathed, lifting the beautiful work of art from the box to hold it up to herself. It was a perfect fit by the look of it. Harper carefully returned the dress to the box and grabbed the invitation.

"You are cordially invited to the private wedding of Ms. Vanessa Vermeulen and Mr. Stuart Buck at the Château du Muguet this Saturday. Invitation only."

Harper blinked back tears of genuine happiness for Vanessa and Stuart as she stared at the invitation. She shouldn't go but she wanted to.

She wanted to watch at least two people join in marriage for all the right reasons.

Vanessa didn't care about Stuart's money—Harper had since found out, Vanessa had her own cash—and Stuart was over the moon for his sassy lady.

That was how love was supposed to work.

It wasn't calculated or manipulated.

It just happened.

Like a wildflower pushing its way through the dirt to find the sun.

Suddenly, Harper was sobbing uncontrollably, crushing the invitation in her hand as she dropped to her knees.

Why couldn't she let herself fall in love?

Why couldn't she trust that not all men were like Rex? That her fate wasn't going to be the same as Anna's?

Harper desperately wanted to believe that things could be different. She wanted to believe that she didn't have to lower herself to sleep with men she cared nothing for just to survive.

Hell, she wanted to believe that she could stop the punishing workouts and enjoy an order of cheesy fries without worrying that men will stop finding her attractive if she softened around the middle.

No, that was bullshit. If she were being honest, she wanted *one* man to feel that way about her.

One man to tell her all those things.

One man to love her unconditionally.

One man...

And his name was Teagan Carmichael.

The doorbell rang again and Harper scrambled to her feet with the desperate hope that it might be Teagan standing on the other side but when she saw another courier, she nearly started crying all over again.

Flowers.

She thanked the courier and opened the small card.

To my sex kitten, my dreams are filled with you. See you soon.

Harper groaned and ripped the card to shreds. Then, because she wasn't satisfied with simply destroying the words, she stomped on the flowers with all the rage and disappointment she couldn't voice.

She didn't want Vincent.

Heaven help her, if that man tried to touch her again, she'd stab his beefy little fingers with a shrimp fork.

That tiny voice of reason told her to *get a grip*. Throwing a temper tantrum wasn't going to solve anything. Neither was pining for a man who wasn't meant to be hers.

Should she go to the wedding?

Her gaze strayed to the dress.

It looked hand sewn.

Stuart and Vanessa had gone to great trouble to provide her with a beautiful dress to wear to the wedding.

She didn't want to insult either of them.

But…how would she manage to put Vincent off for a week while she attended a wedding Teagan might be attending?

A sudden thrill tickled her insides—a wild jump of adrenaline that she could neither control nor stop—and she knew that seeing Teagan again was the worst thing to do if she wanted to stick to her plan.

Could she see Teagan without falling straight into his bed?

Her gaze strayed to the dress.

What would Teagan say to her if he saw her again?

Probably nothing nice.

Maybe he wouldn't come.

Maybe he wasn't invited.

But chances were high that if Stuart and Vanessa invited her, they'd extended the same invite to Teagan.

She worried her bottom lip.

Harper wanted to go.

A voice warned, *Don't go*.

Tears crowded her eyes again.

Just one more time.

I swear it'll be enough.

She just wanted to see Teagan once more and then she'd close the book on whatever feelings remained.

Releasing a shaky breath, she allowed a tremulous smile at the possibility that Teagan might be at the wedding.

If fate wanted it so, he would be there.

If not, that seemed a pretty damning indication that they were never meant to cross paths in the first place.

Honestly, she didn't know which outcome she was hoping for.

25

TEAGAN ARRIVED AT the swanky Château du Muguet and allowed the sharply dressed valet to park his car.

He straightened his tuxedo, pulling the minute wrinkles from the fine cloth, before heading inside.

The air was clean—a sharp difference from the usual Los Angeles muck that clogged the skies—but Big Bear Lake was a far cry from the crowded city.

Teagan was ushered down an expansive hallway, his dress shoes clicking as he went, to a private room where the groom's party was supposed to be hiding out until given the green light to start the processional.

But as Teagan entered the room, he saw only Stuart, dressed neatly in a fine black tuxedo, nervously adjusting his cuff links. Stuart broke into a warm smile as Teagan entered, gesturing for him to come and join him.

"Where's the rest of your party?" he asked, confused. "Am I too early?"

"You're perfectly on time," Stuart reassured Teagan. Then he turned to face Teagan, chin lifted high for his assessment. "How do I look?"

"You look great," Teagan said with a puzzled smile. "But I'm a little confused…"

"Ah, right, yes, about that… Vanessa and I only wanted

the people who meant the most to us to share in our special day. It was only fitting that we invite you and Harper to join our children for our wedding. Vanessa's daughter and my two sons are here as well. I think you'll really get on with them. Good people."

Teagan could only nod as the import of what Stuart had shared rolled over him. "Harper?" he repeated. "Did she come?"

"Yes."

"She's here?" The breath felt stuck in his lungs. "Does she know that I'm here?"

"I doubt it. She's cloistered away with my beautiful bride."

Teagan nodded, his mouth suddenly dry. "Do you have something I could drink? Water? Beer? Anything?"

Stuart chuckled and pointed to the minifridge. "Help yourself."

Harper.

He'd known there was a slight possibility that she might come, but honestly, he'd talked himself into accepting that Harper wouldn't.

And now that he was faced with the realization that he was about to see her again, he couldn't stop shaking.

Great, maybe he had the flu.

Another sharply dressed person politely informed Stuart that they were ready to begin and Stuart drew himself up to his full stature, looking happier than any man had a right to be.

"Are you ready?" Stuart asked.

Teagan chuckled weakly. "Isn't that my line?"

"Son, I've already done this once before. I know what I'm doing and I have no regrets. She's the one. Through thick and thin and whatever time we have left on this planet, Vanessa is my other half. And I can't wait to get on with it."

Stuart made it sound so eloquently simple.

But life wasn't that uncomplicated.

Or maybe it was.

Hell, he didn't know anymore.

"You're a good man," Teagan choked out, not sure if he was choking on his own emotion or the admiration he had for Stuart.

Stuart grinned and patted Teagan's face. "Let's do this," he said, placing the ring in Teagan's hand for safekeeping. "My bride awaits."

Outside in the garden, a beautiful bower filled with autumn flowers framed a brilliant evening sky.

The officiant awaited beneath the bower.

Teagan and Stuart took their places alongside two grown men Teagan assumed were Stuart's sons, opposite a pretty young lady who must've been Vanessa's daughter and folded their hands to wait expectantly for the bride and her maid of honor.

The music started and Teagan held his breath.

Harper entered first.

Her dark hair was twisted in a messy knot of curls with tiny sprays of baby's breath woven in the thick mass, and she looked a vision in an off-white gown that flowed down her body and pooled delicately at her peep-toed feet.

He thought he would pass out from holding his breath.

She was a vision.

The sun backlit her dark hair giving her an ethereal glow that made his heart beat in time with the murmur of a single name: Harper.

Harper met his gaze and sparks ignited between them—the weeks disappeared and it was as if they'd just spent the night entwined in each other's arms.

In all his life, he'd never loved a woman like he loved Harper.

He'd been avoiding that realization—fighting against it tooth and nail—but seeing her now, he knew it was hopeless.

Harper was his.

And he was hers.

That unspoken message, seared across their hearts in tandem, each knowing in that moment, that there was no running from what they were feeling.

Not ever again.

Come what may, Teagan wasn't leaving without Harper. And she knew it.

Harper saw it in his eyes—the unending promise Teagan's heart declared with each beat.

And he saw in Harper's the tremulous acceptance of what neither could explain nor live without.

His heart cried, *Be mine*.

And her heart answered, *Always*.

There, in the Château du Muguet at someone else's wedding, Teagan had found his bride.

Damn, if that didn't sound like a fairy tale—one that he would spend the rest of his life telling to anyone who would listen.

Because he was one lucky son of a bitch.

Epilogue

HARPER STARED AT the letter in her hand, unable to quite comprehend what she was reading.

Anna had passed weeks after Stuart and Vanessa's wedding, quietly slipping away, her suffering at an end.

Harper had been grateful for Teagan's support throughout as Anna's passing had been more difficult emotionally than she'd been prepared for.

But she certainly couldn't have imagined that Anna would've managed to write what she was reading right now.

Anna must've written the letter before she'd lost function in her hands and the fact that she could hear her mother's voice in her head as she read, caused tears to flow.

My dearest Harper,
You are my greatest success and my biggest heartache. I failed you in life by not teaching you what true love looks like but I didn't realize what I was looking for until it was too late. My love for you was the purest love I could ever imagine experiencing.

If you're reading this, I'm gone.

I wish I had been more of a mother when I was alive, one you could count on, but we are dealt our hand and must live with our decisions.

Somehow, in my ignorance, I gave you the wrong message about love.

Love is kind, generous and compassionate.

It yields with grace and sings with joy.

I know this because whenever I looked at you... I felt it.

I'm sorry I never got the chance to show you properly what it means to love.

The reality is that my death is the only blessing I can offer you.

Please take this money and carve a beautiful life for yourself.

All my love,
Mom

Tears blinded Harper as the paper shook in her hands. She looked to Teagan, unable to read any further. He helped her, grasping the paperwork and reading it for her.

Finished, he looked to Harper and said, "Your mom left you as the beneficiary of her life insurance. It's a tidy sum of money."

"What?" Harper wiped at her eyes, confused. "What are you talking about?"

"Seems your mom found an insurance company willing to take her on, in spite of her illness. She must've been early in her diagnosis. She knew she was going to die eventually and she wanted to be there for you in some way."

Harper broke down and sobbed. This whole time she'd never known.

All the times she'd unfairly judged her mother for decisions that couldn't be changed, for a past that wouldn't die because Harper nursed that anger to feed her justifications—the unfairness of Harper's judgment clogged her throat with misery.

Teagan gathered her in his arms and she wept her eyes out.

She didn't know how long she cried, but Teagan's warmth curled around her, holding her tight, and enabled her to get through.

"That was an incredibly selfless thing for your mom to do," Teagan told her softly. "She loved you very much."

Harper nodded against his chest, still unable to believe she'd been completely unaware. "She must've known how I was paying for her care," she realized with a sad hiccup, feeling foolish for assuming her mother hadn't been smart enough to figure it out. "I feel terrible."

"Don't," he said firmly, releasing her so he could meet her gaze. "Your mom knew you were doing the best that you could do and that's why she did this—to show you that she understood and wanted to make up for so much in the only way she could."

Teagan was right. Harper nodded and wiped at her eyes. "It's a lot of money," she said, still in shock. "What should I do with it?"

"Whatever you like," he answered without hesitation. "It's your money."

Since Teagan had started working for Stuart and Vanessa, his income had hit the stratosphere. They were more than comfortable and still enjoyed the perks of traveling wherever they liked on Stuart's private jet.

"I want to make a donation to MS research," she decided. "Not all of it, but a good portion. The rest I'll invest. I know she would've liked that."

Teagan brushed a kiss across her lips, so tender and loving. She gazed up at him, wondering how she ever thought she could live without him.

Teagan was her touchstone, her lover, confidante and best friend.

All this time she'd thought love was an illusion, a game made for suckers.

Now, Harper realized, love was the only thing that lived on when all else had turned to dust.

Her heart had known all along what her brain wouldn't accept.

Love made life worth living.

* * * * *

*If you loved this novel, don't miss other titles
by Kimberly Van Meter available at Harlequin.com!*

Get 2 Free Books,
Plus 2 Free Gifts—
just for trying the Reader Service!

*Captain Nolee Arnauyq has never wanted or needed
to be rescued. Until her crab fishing boat is caught
in a violent storm and gorgeous Coast Guard rescue
swimmer Dylan Holt lands on her deck.*

*Read on for a sneak preview of
HIS LAST DEFENSE,
the latest Karen Rock title from the series
UNIFORMLY HOT!*

"We have one minute," he heard his commander say
through his helmet's speakers. "Is your captain ready?
Over?"

"She will be," Dylan answered. He slung an arm over
a rope line and held fast when another swell lifted him
off his feet. The ship groaned as sheets of metal strained
against each other like fault lines before an earthquake.
The lashings clanked. "Send down the strop. Over."

"You have fifty seconds and then I want you on deck,
Holt," barked his commander.

Dylan shoved his way along the slick deck, propelling
himself across its steep slant. "Roger that."

He would get Nolee out. End of story.

Descending as fast as he dared, he fought the wind
and dropped down into the hull again. Icy water made his
breath catch even with the benefit of the dry suit. Nolee
should have been out of here long before now.

"I've almost got it." Her strained voice emerged from blue lips. Her movements were jerky as she twisted wire around the still gushing pipe. She was losing motor function. Hypothermia was already setting in.

"It's over, Nolee. Come with me now."

When she opened her mouth, her head lolled. Her eyelids dropped. Reacting on instinct, he grabbed her limp form before she crumpled into the freezing water.

He hauled her out of the hull and across the deck where a rescue strop dangled. Damn, damn, damn. His hands weren't cooperating, his own motor function feeling the effects of the cold. Once he'd tethered them together, he gave his flight mechanic a thumbs-up. The boat flung them sideways, careening over the rail.

Swinging, their feet skimmed the deadly swells. The line jerked them up through the stinging air. He tightened his arms around her. With only a tether connecting her to him, he couldn't lose his grip.

As they rose, he forced himself not to look at her. He'd dreamed about that face too many times, even after he left Kodiak to forget her.

But he wouldn't be doing his job if he didn't hold her close. And heaven help him—no matter how much she'd gutted him nine years ago—he couldn't deny she felt damned good in his arms.

Don't miss
HIS LAST DEFENSE by Karen Rock,
available April 2017 wherever
Harlequin® Blaze® books and ebooks are sold.

www.Harlequin.com